OPALINE ALLANDET

Quentin the Rebel

Contents

To Michel Berthelin, to whom I am thankful for his friendly support.

"*Revenge* squeezes the heart as tightly as the *jaw.*"
Charles de Leusse

Foreword

This book is the sequel to *Godefroy the Cruel*, which was published in 2014. Although the characters are fictional, the story takes place in a real historical context—that of the Holy Roman Empire during the Middle Ages—which I have studied extensively. Burgundy was part of the Empire during this time period.

I intentionally focused on the difficult position of being a woman. At this time, women existed only in the shadows of men (husbands, fathers, brothers, uncles, etc.), even among aristocrats. Historians have told us little about the women's status, as the historians themselves were men.... Moreover, I have considered the fact that, during the Middle Ages, the Catholic Church reigned supreme, and that popes often were seen as more than kings. Thus, religion played an important role in medieval society.

1

Isadora of Willeim

On a radiant morning in June 1197, Godefroy of Lanicey, known as 'Godefroy the Cruel,' sent his driver to prepare a carriage to bring him to the castle of Vauzelle, where resided the Duke of Sacht. The carriage was pulled by two horses. The baron was accompanied by three of his men; as a nobleman, never traveled alone.

As he intended to stay there for several days, he ordered the chambermaid to gather all his belongings in a trunk. He had taken great care of his physical appearance: his black hair, powdered with a few white hairs, was freshly cut, as was his beard. He was dressed in a long, light tunic of beige linen, which fell onto his black breeches. A big man, he was still strong for his age; he cut a fine figure when he entered the wide driveway leading to the castle of Vauzelle.

As he walked on, he thought, once more, that his own fortress was more impressive, and he found himself rejoicing in the fact. Recognizing him, the guards let him cross the drawbridge.

He tugged on the bell that hung beside the gate. A servant opened the door and bowed before him. "Enter, my lord!"

Then, suddenly, the Baron's son-in-law, Othon of Sacht, ran up to meet him: "Ah! You're finally among us, my friend!" He shook Godefroy's hand warmly. "We welcome you to the castle. Make yourself comfortable. You must be tired."

"No!" replied the baron. "I still carry myself well."

Lidwine was in an adjoining room, busy rocking her child. Upon recognizing her father's gruff voice, she took the infant in her arms and held him to her bosom. Softly, she murmured, "Your grandfather has arrived, and I must introduce you to him. I hope, my dear, you won't look like him—he's a bad man."

When her father arrived, however, the young woman kissed him cordially and introduced him to little Conrad.

"Is our son not absolutely delightful?" Othon asked; he was very proud of their child.

"Yes, he's a beautiful baby!" Godefroy—who was searching for the eyes of Isadora, his friend's cousin—assured her.

Indeed, the young widow had appeared at the back of the room; she wanted to remain inconspicuous.

"Come closer, dear lady," exclaimed the sire. "Let me admire you more closely."

Isadora blushed slightly, which enhanced her natural charm. Then, she walked to Godefroy.

"Allow me, Madame, to kiss your hand. You're simply exquisite!"

"You may call me 'Isadora'," she said, after bowing to him.

"All in good time! I'm quite flattered."

The Marquise of Willeim, who was thirty-two years old, looked younger than she was. Like almost all the Alsatians, she wore her hair in a thick blond plait that emerged from behind her cap. Her round, graceful face was complemented by milky skin that showed no wrinkles. She was well-proportioned, with a slim waist that enhanced her feminine curves—curves which Godefroy found rather appetizing. He also found that—although

2

she was not as beautiful as Mahaut, his first wife, had been in her youth—this woman was very charming, and he felt like she had captured his heart.

"I've been told you are a widow. I wonder why a woman as lovely as you has not yet remarried."

Irritated by her father's gallant comments, Lidwine left the room. She was outraged: she could not forget the long, odious martyrdom he had inflicted upon her innocent mother. This torture had resulted in the death of the latter. Poor Mahaut had been weakened and destroyed by so much cruelty![1]

The next day—as the weather promised to be radiant—Othon proposed to Godefroy and his cousin that they ride around the castle in his own carriage.

Sitting beside Isadora, the baron breathed in her sweet violet perfume, and he was exhilarated. The hilly landscape of this county was scattered with steep hills and many curves—curves which, when they passed over them, caused Isadora to be thrown against the sire, much to the latter's delight. Then, he took the opportunity to hold her arm so that it was less shaken by the movement. On her end, the young woman seemed to appreciate this protective gesture. He could tell—not only because she did not withdraw her arm, but also because she moved closer to him....

They followed a towpath running along a winding river, and returned via a popular trail. A light breeze caressed them pleasantly as they passed. This ride was proving to be delicious.

The Duke of Sacht was delighted to notice that a tender sort of intimacy was developing between his two guests.

Back at the castle, the marquise withdrew to hers room to rest

---

[1] See *Godefroy the Cruel* (2014).

for a moment. There, she reflected on recent events. Her cousin had extolled the baron's bravery and good education. She knew that his fortress was impressive, and that many estates depended on it. But her own fortune, inherited from her late husband, was enough. No, what she dreamed of was flourishing alongside a brave lord, loyal and faithful, who would know how to protect her. Furthermore, her son Karl, aged ten, would benefit from the model of a true knight, seeing as he no longer had a father. Now, Baron Lanicey seemed to possess the virtues she desired. If the sire did end up asking her hand in marriage, Isadora thought, she would not refuse.

Meanwhile, in the parlor, the two friends had gathered to discuss together.

Othon asked Godefroy about his son. "Do you regret Quentin's departure? He could have said goodbye before he enlisted in our emperor's army."

"No. In truth, his departure didn't cause me pain. Our personalities are too different. He was acting neither submissive enough, nor reasonable enough, for us to agree. I'm still holding a grudge against him."

"Really? Why is that?"

"Because he refused the wealthy wedding I organized for him with Bertille Attrans, the daughter of one of my neighbors and friends. Negotiations with the Marquis of Attrans had been favorable until that point. Bertille herself seemed delighted. Our lands are connected as well. It would have strengthened our fortune and our status among other lords, and even potentially with the Duke of Burgundy. But no—he refused!"

"Do you know why he insulted you like that?"

"Yes. It's because he was in love with Aliénor of Scéry and wanted to marry her instead. It's true that this girl was exceptionally beautiful. But, before her father died, he entrusted her to me, and Aliénor was mine.[2]

"Did she love you in return?"

"You should know, dear Othon, because my son should have told you."

The Duke of Sacht—who did know the truth—preferred to hide the fact that he had supported Quentin's cause. If he'd known the truth, Godefroy would have denied it on the spot and accused him of treason! He knew too well how impetuous his friend was.

"I think she must be, since Quentin ran away with her. I found this out through my messenger; he's friends with Wilfried, one of your old servants. The most terrible thing, though, is that Aliénor was murdered soon after. I wonder who could have wanted her dead—she was such a good person!"

"Yes, me too," Godefroy lied calmly.

"And I suppose we will never get hands on the culprit...."

"Certainly not."

The Baron judged that he ought to close this line of discussion, so he switched the topic to politics. "According to the rumors, a fourth Crusade is on its way. Do you know if it will truly take place?"

"No," replied Othon, "nothing is definite. But I think we will have to avenge our valiant comrades, who were savagely massacred while fighting on our side just a few years ago."

"I agree with you. But it appears that our Emperor, Henry VI, decided to lead it."

"In that case, your son will participate, and he'll have the chance to demonstrate his bravery."

At that moment, Isadora and Lidwine crossed the room on their

---

[2] See *Godefroy the Cruel* (2014).

way to the garden. The Marquise offered to accompany them; they accepted eagerly.

Godefroy had been staying with his daughter for ten days, and, even though it was raining a lot, he decided to return home.

"But why can't you stay here longer?" the Duke said, after having pulled him aside.

"I must watch my properties, even though Ulric—in whom I trust completely—is very competent. In fact, he's better at it than I."

"Were you able to form an opinion regarding my cousin, even though you haven't been here long?"

"Of course! I have a lot of experience and expertise with women, and I can assure you that my choice has been made."

His friend was stunned for a moment, until he remembered that he himself had fallen for Lidwine as soon as he had seen her portrait. "ay I know your decision?"

"Don't worry about it. You'll be able to hear it once I leave."

Throughout all of lunch—which was served outside, under a rose arbor, as it was still nice out—Othon appeared somewhat nervous, as he feared a refusal on the baron's part. But the latter—who was greedily swallowing the desserts and poultry dishes brought forth by a servant—remained imperturbable. As for Isadora, she seemed sad when Godefroy announced his upcoming departure. Inwardly, she reflected angrily on her inability to make him understand her interest in him. She remained silent, though, barely listening to conversations that still focused on the political situation of the Holy Roman Empire, and bit her lips. Her attitude did not escape the perceptive eyes of the malicious sire, who was rejoicing over his own victories. He had reached his goal. So when he got up, having savoured the last drops of excellent regional liquor, the marquise was still absorbed in thought.

It was at that point that Godefroy walked toward her, and—after having majestically bowed to her—he told her, "Madam, I am deeply honored to ask for your hand. Will you marry me?"

Right then, at that precise moment, Isadora wondered if she was dreaming. Then, upon realizing that this proposal was indeed addressed to her, the young woman said, with a dazzling smile, "Oh, my lord! You have me very happy! Yes, I accept your proposal."

Othon cried out in joy. On her end, Lidwine was content simply to congratulate them. In truth, she feared that her friend would become as unhappy as her late mother has been. But she had no choice but to keep this secret to herself.

The Duke rang a bell to call his servant forth. "Corentin, bring us more good wine. We will soon need to quench our thirst!"

The Holy Roman Empire was, in June of 1197, led by Henry VI, the eldest son of Frederick Barbarossa. In French, he was dubbed 'Henry the Severe' because of his brutal and warlike temperament; indeed, he never hesitated to kill those around him. At twenty, his father had married Constance de Hauteville, a Duchess of Burgundy. His son, Frederick II, was born in 1194. Named King of the Romans in 1169, Henry was crowned king of Italy in 1186. He sought to seize Sicily, and so he imprisoned Richard the Lionheart, King of England, in a fort. He extracted a large ransom from the English before finally releasing him. Then, he eliminated the ruler of Sicily by making him sit on a white-hot throne. Next, he sequestered Queen Sybil of Sicily, as well as her three daughters. As for their son, who was only a child, Henry had his eyes put out. Finally, not content with having killed the priest, Henry had his body exhumed from his grave so that it could be beheaded. He also had the Bishop of Liège murdered in 1192. As his cruelty had made him many enemies, both within and outside the Empire, he could not maintain the peace that had existed in Germany during his father's reign. Many German princes rose up against him, and they divided themselves into two rival clans: Clan Hohenstaufen (his own) and Clan Brunswick.

Godefroy of Lanicey wasted no time. As soon as he returned to his fortress, he asked to meet with Ulric, who was his constant accomplice—even when times were tough—and to whom he now explained his intentions.

"Ulric, since you have become my main confidant, I must inform you of my recent decision."

"I'm listening to you, Master."

The soulless old man waited for Godefroy to indicate a seat to him before sitting down. His face was so wrinkled that his precise age could not easily be deduced, though he must have been older than forty. He had allowed his beard and moustache to grow long; at the moment, they were concealing an evil grin.

"Well, I'll be brief: I shall soon marry again."

Ulric did not even raise an eyebrow; he was well accustomed to hiding his opinions. In this instance, however, he was not surprised. "Have you ever found another damsel who's as beautiful as she was?" he asked. But as he knew the sire perfectly well, he did not refer to Aliénor, as she no longer existed in his eyes.

"You are quite correct," Godefroy said, rubbing his hands together. "But this time, I will marry with a wealthy widow, the Marquise of her estate. And for that reason, I ask that you order everyone who works here to clean the castle so completely that not even a single speck of dust can be seen."

"It will be done, sir. I'd just like to know when your wedding will take place."

"In three weeks, so there's enough time to prepare all the festivities."

Ulric, who never wasted an opportunity to drink, waited for a moment, in case the sire should propose a toast. He looked mischievously in the direction of the secret cupboard, which contained many fine bottles of wine. Godefroy immediately understood this signal; he turned around and took out a bottle of a wine that was from their own terroir.

"Come on, let's toast to my new love!" he cried, laughing joyfully.

"Yes, indeed, Master, and I hope that you'll amuse yourself greatly!" replied Ulric, whose laughter creaked like an old spinning wheel.

Then, he dared to probe further: "Should I watch her discreetly, as I did with Lady Mahaut?"

"No. It will not be necessary because that lady there, beautiful as she is, will not attract as much attention as did that bitch who's thankfully rotting underground. She doesn't have the same insolent beauty as Aliénor did."

The man without a soul was careful not to comment on the murdered girl. It was as if he had never known her.

And again, they pealed with rich laughter. They even chatted about rents and yield of the land.

Godefroy was in an excellent mood. He was sitting comfortably in his chair at the top of the tower where his office was located. He had become the undisputed, indisputable leader of this fortress. His son could no longer wield power over him.

News of the baron's remarriage spread like wildfire among all the servants of the fortress, even though this was forbidden, under pain of being hanged—an allusion to the death of Mahaut, his late wife.[3] The marquise could not know a single thing about this matter.

Many of the female servants, who had been recently hired, rejoiced at the idea of serving this magnificent unknown lady. This dark castle would finally come alive, as the sire would organize celebrations to show off his new wife for the other lords of the county. The older servants, including Hildegarde and her daughters, reacted to this decision with less alacrity. They bitterly recalled the previous baroness, whose immense beauty had led her to her grave—but they vowed to keep silent about it.

On the other hand, when their master informed them that this widow had a ten-year-old son, they were delighted. A child—young and enthusiastic and careless—might iron out some of their problems. And he would no doubt remind them of Quentin, that beloved child who had grown up and disappeared, six months ago now.

Every day, Hildegarde went to the castle's small chapel and prayed fervently to the Virgin, so that She could bring Quentin back to her. She missed the young man so much! At night-time, when she was convinced that nobody could see her, she crept over to the pile of dirt that that was covered Mahaut's remains. She also prayed for his late mistress's soul to rest, and let some tears escape from her....

When Isadora of Willeim, accompanied by her son Karl, crossed the two drawbridges that protected the imposing fortress of Lanicey, she felt intimidated. And, though she didn't quite know why, a fearful chill ran down her spine. She had to go to his apartment while completely covered up, with even her

_____

[3] See *Godefroy the Cruel* (2014).

10

face veiled—and all because no one should see her before the wedding.

This was because Godefroy wanted to completely surprise his subordinates, as well as those people who made their living off his estate. Furthermore, an old legend, which had been transmitted orally from generation to generation, suggested that, if the bride was seen before the wedding celebration, this would bring him bad luck. Only Hildegarde had seen her, when she'd been in the hallway that led to her room, believing herself alone. But the old servant, who had hidden so that she could watch them, judged her less beautiful than Mahaut had been, and was relieved for it.

The priest who was to officiate the marriage came to the baron to prepare for the ceremony, but the latter flatly refused. "My good priest, how dare you suggest that we make such a fuss when you've known for a long time that I do not believe in your God?" he said.

"But, lord, you must obey Pope Innocent III; he demands that the sacrament of marriage be celebrated. Otherwise, you will never taste the joys of Paradise!"

"What do I care about Paradise? I simply ask you to bless the rings and the nuptial bed so that this union may be fruitful. That seems to be the most important part of marriage."

"I understand that; the Church accepts the marriage, especially since it has the purpose of procreation."

"And I intend to once again father a son!" Godefroy added.

"All in due time!" the priest rejoiced.

The day of the wedding—it was celebrated on July 30th, 1197—was quite memorable. The sun was shining abundantly, and all the guests rejoiced in its warmth. The subjects had also been invited to the festivities. In the streets, the music of flutes rang through the air, and a group of clowns danced over to the castle. In addition, a huge table was mounted on trestles in one corner.

Next, all the guests, arranged by rank, sat at the table when the horn sounded. The servants, who were very numerous, busied themselves preparing dishes and slicing meat. The meat came mostly from pigs raised at the castle, as well from game animals hunted down by its denizens. The meats were accompanied by carrots, beets, beans and peas, all of them rather spicy. The peals of horns echoed each time a new dish was served. Behind the castellans stood the artisans and peasants who had been given the opportunity to feast with the others. They were making a big fuss, and had to be scolded.

The lords and ladies, however, proved more worthy; they did not neglect to congratulate Baron Lanicey. Isadora was immediately surrounded by noble ladies offering her their friendship; she was touched at their kindness. Everyone admired her wedding dress: a long, pale blue silk gown, interwoven with gold threads. Her blond hair, which was enclosed in a large white veil, still managed to light up her face. Her adopted son looked impressive in his brand-new clothes as well. Young though he was, he already had the countenance of a fine young nobleman.

The wedding night was wondrous for both spouses, even though the Church frowned on sexual activity, even between spouses. Godefroy was not disappointed when he undressed his wife: although she was not curvaceous, her breasts were in full blossom, and they were still firm. He took the time to admire them before enjoying the pleasures of her hot, soft body. And as Isadora dared to reveal her sensual side, her pleasure increased tenfold.

Some two months later, while the sire was ransacking the archives in his study, he suddenly heard an unusual commotion in the lower parts of his fortress: the neighing of horses, mixed with the voices of men. Getting to his feet, he ran up the tower to check that no one was attacking the castle. Instead, he recognized an emissary of the kingdom; the man was accompanied by three other riders. What could be happening?

Godefroy ordered the guards to raise the drawbridge and let the men pass through. He received them in the armory, which was located on the ground floor.

The Count of Poix, who had been dispatched by a prince, saluted the baron. "Good morning, sir. In my capacity as leader of the fief, I must inform you that Emperor Henry VI was killed on September 28th, during a battle in Messina, Sicily."

Initially, Godefroy was stunned, but he quickly regained his senses. "Can it be? He was only thirty-two. And who will govern us now?"

"For now, we simply don't know. I believe that, before he participated in the Fourth Crusade, the emperor had appointed his brother, the Duke of Swabia, as regent. But nothing is for sure yet."

"I think we will soon plunge into a civil war, since several major German princes will now claim access to the throne."

"The thought scares me deeply," replied the count.

"Personally, I won't regret his death; he was too bloodthirsty, and thought only of crushing everything in his path. He did not have as much range as his father, either—that man made our empire the largest kingdom in Europe."

The Count of Poix continued delivering his news. "Our lord has instructed me to inform you of this because he would welcome your support in promoting the election of Philip of Swabia. He knows that you are a true leader."

He was not wrong. In fact, Godefroy had once harangued the knights of the neighboring kingdom to participate in the Third Crusade.

"I am very flattered!" Godefroy said now. "Tell him that he can count on me."

After the four riders had left, Godefroy reflected for a moment. He thought that Germany was about to enter a period of crisis, of conflict. Frederick II, the only son of Henry VI, was but three years old; a regent needed to be found.

Godefroy took the liberty of warning all the neighboring gentry, via the intermediary of Ulric, who had somehow become his right-hand man since Quentin's departure. He also addressed a letter to his son-in-law and friend, the Duke of Sacht, as he knew that the latter shared his opinions.

Isadora didn't find the news particularly important, as she had little interest in politics. She sought instead to please the inhabitants of the fortress, as well as their close neighbors. She also had to ensure the education of her son, so she sent for a tutor, who could continue his education in arithmetic and grammar.

Karl was a lovely, keenly intelligent child who already knew the rules of etiquette. He immediately befriended a young page, Hugues de Chassiniat, to whom Godefroy was training in the military arts. Hugues was being trained so that he could succeed his father, himself a leader of a major stronghold in the county of Autun. Although Hugues was two years older than Karl, he was hardly bigger than his young friend. He worked in the fortress; Karl, who had idle time, accompanied him. He followed his friend to the stables, where he cleaned the horses' coats, and to the well, where he fetched water.

Karl also went with the young page to the visit the village forge.

Here, they learned how horseshoes were manufactured. With a kind of punching motion of his hammer, the blacksmith pierced holes for square nails into the red iron. He then fashioned four irons with the dimensions of a hoof. Once the iron had taken on a flat shape, he knocked four or five points into the edges of the iron so as to form small ledges. Then, he drew down a small portion of the metal clamp around the horseshoe. He then crimped several nails, which were planted across the horseshoe, onto the sides of the shoe.

Karl was amazed by what he discovered at Hugue's side. "I want to see what life is like outside the fortress!" he said upon seeing his friend head in the direction of the surrounding villages.

"You shouldn't envy me, I assure you. Very often, I have to do tasks that could be done by servants. Sometimes I even feel like a lackey. But I dare not say anything because the baron, your stepfather, won't spare me."

"Really? Why is that?"

"Because he believes that, in order to become a good leader, you must already know how to obey."

Karl's eyes popped wide open. He had never heard comments like these before. "Is he hard on you?"

"'Hard' is not the right word. He is ruthless, both with me and with all those in his service." For a moment, Hugues became fearful; he bit his lip. "But promise me you won't say anything. He would dismiss me if he knew what I've said."

"Yes, I swear that I won't, since we're friends."

Despite his words, however, the boy could not help discussing it covertly with his mother later on.

"No, darling," Isadora exclaimed, "please don't believe everything you hear in the castle! All servants complain about their masters, but they still have to treat him with respect. Do you understand?"

"Yes, Mother," he said, agreeing with her so that he wouldn't upset her.

The new Baroness Lanicey did not attach much importance to this exchange; since her marriage, she had been overjoyed. Everyone saw her as a lady of noble lineage, and no one ventured to contradict her. After all, was she not the sire's wife?

The sire was proud to be married to such a beautiful lady, but he became even prouder when, one sunny day in autumn, she declared, "My dear husband, next spring, you will be a father." Modest as she was, she could not stop herself from blushing during her confession.

"Is it possible, my love? We've only been married for three months."

"That's true. But God has blessed our union; it has borne fruit."

"By Jove, yes! I've never had relations with a woman as passionate as you. Look how well I've been rewarded!"

"And I thought that I could not bear children! Imagine my joy at finding out."

"Why do you say that?"

"Because my late husband gave me only one child. I thought I had become barren."

Godefroy was still incredulous. "But are you sure you're pregnant? I'll fetch a matron to confirm it."

"Yes, I'd be most thankful."

He did not address the old matron who had once examined Mahaut, but rather a woman from a nearby village, who was renowned for her skills.

The sire had his driver fetch her, and he ordered the driver to make her come in by the back of the fortress. He insisted that the visit be kept secret so as to avoid unnecessary gossip among the servants. When she arrived, the matron spoke to Isadora, fingered her breasts and belly—which she found suitably hard—and then examined her closely. Standing outside the room, Godefroy waited impatiently for them to finish.

At last, the matron came out, satisfied. "Congratulations, sir! Your wife is indeed pregnant, but, given her advanced age, she'll need to rest often. Give her a little red wine every day, and have her eat quince and eggs. All of this will strengthen her. And remember: she should not travel on horseback."

"Don't worry," he reassured her, delighted. "I will watch her closely."

"Yes, giving birth is a blessing from Heaven—especially at that age!"

"I know."

After she had left, Godefroy almost sank into the door of the bedroom. Quickly kissing his wife, he said, "Dearest Isadora, thanks to you, I feel twenty years younger. My eldest son no longer exists for me, since he left without a word, and I'd be happy never to see him again."

The young woman was deeply touched. "Ah! If only I could give you a son to succeed you at the castle! It would be my greatest joy."

"In a few years, Karl will be able to reign over the fortress of Willeim. At the moment, it's under my brother's rule."

Godefroy was overjoyed by their declaration of love. On the one hand, he was very proud of his manhood, as he could still beget children at forty-two years old. However, during the county months of pregnancy, he vowed to keep the upcoming birth a secret.

2

Guillaume of Lanicey

As he had promised to the Count of Poix, the baron commissioned his best rider to accompany the sires who lived in his district. His mission was to inform them of the death of their emperor, and to invite them to meet in the fortress of Lanicey to gather support for the Duke Philip of Swabia, the second son of Frederick Barbarossa.

For his part, Godefroy sent a letter to his son-in-law, the Duke of Sacht, in which he wrote:

Dear friend,

As you may already know, our sovereign Henry V died on September 28th, leaving the throne vacant, as his son Frederick II is too young to rule. Before going to war in Sicily, he appointed his brother Philip ruler of our kingdom. But the Brunswick princes hope to crown Othon IV, who is one of their own, instead.

It seems that we must support Philip of Swabia against his rival. Therefore, I'm organizing a meeting for those from neighboring fortresses; it is to be held at Lanicey, on October the 10th.

It is my pleasure to invite you to the meeting, as I know you share my opinion. We hope you join us soon.

Sincerely,

Godefroy of Lanicey

On October 10th, 1197, Godefroy received, in his office at the top of the keep, the Marquis of Attrans—with whom he had reconciled after Quentin's departure—as well as Count Antoine of Fouchardière and the Viscount of Palindrey, two lords from the neighboring lands. The Duke of Sacht had followed his father-in-law's orders by gathering the two men. Not many supporters had gathered at Lanicey, however; the other invitees had preferred to abstain. There was no doubt that they preferred to support Philip's rival, Otto of Brunswick.

"My friends," Godefroy began, "although there are very few of us, we'll support Philip of Swabia, whom our late Emperor appointed as regent before he left to conquer to Sicily. Therefore, we must respect his wishes."

"Of course," nodded the other lords.

"This is especially the case since Otto of Brunswick is a descendant of the throne of England by his mother," Godefroy clarified, "who is the daughter of Henry II, and by his uncle Richard Lionheart."

"It belongs to the Welf family," objected the Count of Fouchardière, "which is one of the largest families in Germany."

"Yes, but Frederick Barbarossa deprived his father, Henry the Lion, of his duchies. As a result, Otto was forced into exile in England. And do you know why Otto IV is a candidate for leading the Empire? Because his uncle, Richard Lionheart, needs a German ruler who is allied with him against Philip Augustus, the King of the Franks."

"Therefore," continued the Duke of Sacht, "they believe him unworthy of becoming our next sovereign."

"This can only be achieved through civil war," the Marquis of Attrans reminded them with a sigh, "and for how long? No one knows."

"So what can we do?" inquired the Viscount of Palindrey.

"We can support Philip by providing him with soldiers who we've converted to his cause," Godefroy said. "Also, we have no qualms of creating propaganda to arouse our peoples."

"I will send my sons over there, so they may fight at his side," said the Marquis of Attrans.

"That's an excellent idea, my friend."

The Viscount of Palindrey added, "And I'm lecturing everyone in our villages to encourage them to fight against Otto IV."

"Speak with all your family and friends as well. The more of us there are, the more success we'll have in defeating this usurper."

When the meeting ended, Godefroy rang a large bell to call forth a servant. When one appeared, he bowed several times to the gentlemen, and then waited for orders.

"Go get us the best wine from our beautiful county, and pour us generous portions."

"Very well, Master."

After that—and, especially, after they had drunk the fragrant, palatable red wine—the atmosphere became more relaxed. They spoke of their private lives. The Marquis of Attrans had eventually found a good suitor for his youngest daughter, Béatrix, and everyone congratulated him. Count Antoine of Fouchardière spoke of the many amorous exploits he had carried out, even though he was married. As for the baron of Lanicey, although he did not reveal his wife's pregnancy, they all noticed that he was in a very cheerful humor, and that his character had softened.

The Duke of Sacht wanted to speak to his cousin; he hoped to find her doing well. Entering the castle's main room, he found her sitting with Gerlinde, her usual maid. Gerlinde withdrew so that they could discuss face to face, and he sat down beside Isadora.

"Hello, dear Isadora! How are you?"

"Hello, my dear cousin. As you can see, I'm full of joy."

"Yes, indeed. I am delighted; I can see that you're radiating beauty and health. I would have been much grieved to find that you were unhappily married. But I know my friend well: although he seems rough, you can trust him with complete confidence."

Isadora leaned forward to confide in him. "Godefroy is an excellent husband, and I could never quite praise him enough."

"All in good time!" he said joyously. "But that doesn't surprise me, either. I know how gallant he is. And has your son adapted well to the castle?"

"Oh, yes. Karl has befriended a young page from a very noble family. They sometimes ride horses together. Karl loves horses, and he often accompanies Hugues to the stables."

"Good! It's always ideal for the ruler of a fortress to be a good horseman."

"I hope that you'll spend the night here, seeing as you live very far away."

"Yes, don't worry. I'm only leaving you tomorrow. At the moment, I'm off to congratulate my friend for the good news."

After leaving his cousin, Othon joined Godefroy, who had returned to his office. He told him the secrets Isadora had confided in him, and they spent some time laughing in joy. The Baron was nevertheless extremely flattered by his wife's praise. A good wife must always admire and honor her spouse.

"Ah! Dear Isadora! This is perfect for me, especially since I know that I will always be faithful."

"How can you be sure? You said the same thing about your late wife, Mahaut."

The sire leaped from his seat, striking the table with his fist. "Othon, I forbid you! Do you hear me, I forbid from speaking of this bitch—especially in front of your cousin, who knows nothing of her! Otherwise, I'll be compelled to end our friendship!"

"No, calm down. I would never put our friendship at risk." The Duke hesitated before asking his friend another question. "I don't want to seem rude, but have you heard any news of Quentin?"

"Not at all, and I'm very satisfied for that, since I'm still angry with him. Imagine how ungrateful and unworthy a successor he would have been!"

"What do you mean? Don't you realize that he'll succeed you? Because, one day, he'll end up coming back to you...."

"The later, the better," Godefroy roared, "because I still have not forgiven his arrogance!"

"No!" cried Othon. "That would be a disgrace!"

The Baron was overcome by fury. "And what about me? Have I not been outraged—and, worse than that, hated—by the son who I raised? He went so far as to wage battle with me—me, who gave him life. Fortunately, I was strong enough to defend myself. But how can I accept a son who dared raise a hand against his father?"

Seeing that he was red with anger, Othon did not dare contradict him. "So what will you do?" he asked instead.

"I don't know yet. Now, if you please, do change the subject. How's my little cousin?"

"We found an excellent nurse, and the young chap is greatly enjoying her company."

"That really pleases me! Now, go back to your cousin; I have to leave for work."

And with that, he dismissed him once more.

After six months of incessant fighting between the major rival clans of Hohenstaufen and Brunswick, in March 1198, the princes of the Hohenstaufen party elected Philip of Swabia as king of Germany. Yet Philip—for whom it was intended that he would join the priesthood—became archbishop in 1190, before eventually abandoning the clergy altogether. The second son of Frederick Barbarossa and the brother of Henry VI, he married the daughter of the Byzantine emperor in 1197. None of their sons were born alive, but they had four daughters. Once he had succeeded to the throne, he disappointed Pope Innocent III, whose influence was predominant in Germany. Because he supported his rival Othon IV of Brunswick, this king was therefore never crowned emperor.

In June of 1198, the party of Otto IV, led by the Archbishop of Cologne, elected Othon of Brunswick as king; he was crowned at Aachen. Because the coronation resulted in the election of two kings, a civil war—one which would tear the empire apart over the course of many years—broke out.

Shortly before these events, there were joyful tidings from the castle of Lanicey: the baroness gave birth. When, in the fourth month of pregnancy, Godefroy decided to reveal her condition to his family and friends, everyone was stunned. If the baron was celebrated and praised for his virility, this was not the case for Isadora, who was considered too old to bear children.

Only the priest of the fortress was delighted by this news; the Church held that the first duty of a married woman was to give her husband children. "Noble lady," he said, "God has given you a huge gift. And the Church will be happy to welcome your child, as it should be."

Naturally, it was essential that she gave birth to a boy, who would one day gain the family inheritance. A girl was only important if, through marriage, she brought a sufficient dowry—sufficient, that is, if not downright essential—to her future husband.

Lidwine was shocked; she felt that it was indecent for a child to be born to an older couple. And the prospect of having a half-brother or half-sister greatly displeased her.

For several months, Isadora closed her eyes when those around her whispered about her, and she kept her eyes down while walking in the garden or the village with Gerlinde, her faithful servant. Gerlinde became, for Isadora, a confidante and a friend—someone she truly appreciated. She satisfied her mistress's every whim, never dared to contradict her, and listened to her babbling without letting herself appear weary.

Viscountess Edwige of Palindrey befriended Isadora, and visited her often. The young woman brought her embroidery to Lanicey, and both women chatted as they drew forth their needles. Edwige also brought Isadora cakes made by her cook, and encouraged her to indulge all her sweet cravings. Edwige was thirty years old, and, since she had two daughters of her own, she understood Isadora quite well. She had lost three other young children, including two boys—they had been passed away after a bad fever—and she secretly dreamed of giving birth to yet another son, so as to preserve the legacy of their estate.

Isadora tried to comfort her friend. "You must keep faith; you can still give birth."

"Ah! My dear friend, if only you could tell me the truth! All around me, I've been hearing evil tongues wagging, saying that I have become infertile."

"Don't listen to them. Instead, work hard to please your husband. You're still pretty, and very sweet. Those are the things men prefer in their women. Also, I advise you to pray and make offerings to the Virgin and St. Margaret."

"You really are lovely, and I thank you for your support. Here, have another cake."

One day, Isadora asked Edwige if she knew of a possible nanny for her child.

"I'll look into it," Edwige replied. "I'm happy to find a healthy, well-educated young woman to care for Karl."

"I trust you," said Isadora.

A week later, the Viscountess of Palindrey came to visit her friend, saying that she knew of a young woman who would be delighted to enter into her service.

"In that case, tell me everything!" Isadora said. "Who is she?"

"This young woman has already suffered a great deal, but she is trustworthy. Her name is Clémence of Jaffrerot. She's twenty-five years old, and she has been raising her own child—a four-month-old—on her own.

"Really? What happened?"

"Unfortunately, a married man seduced her, and he told her the truth only after she was expecting."

"Is that true? Maybe he just told her that to get rid of her?"

"Many men would be disgraceful enough for that! Clémence doesn't know any more of this than we do, since this gentleman—if he really was one—disappeared without leaving an address. Can you imagine?"

Isadora concluded that this young woman truly was unfortunate. "How is she managing to raise her baby now?" she asked.

"That's the problem: she lost her mother when she was ten. As for her father, he has no fortune, because he squandered it taking care of his mistresses. That's also why he couldn't marry off his daughter; he had no dowry."

Isadora thought for a moment, and then said, "But, if a woman allowed herself to be seduced without getting married first, then she's at fault. The Church forbids it; everyone knows that. And why didn't she join a convent? Some convents take in women who have sinned."

"She hasn't agreed to give up her child, and I find that admirable."

"That's fair. Many women in that situation would rather place their child in a church than in an orphanage. So, you can introduce to her to me."

This was how Clémence of Jaffrerot was hired. Godefroy, who found her pretty, was in no way opposed to this decision. A thin brunette with blue eyes, a slender figure, even though she had given birth, she was not lacking in charm. Her face was gracious and accommodating, while its translucent complexion confirmed her noble origins. Her forehead, plucked at the roots of her hair, hinted at her coquetry.

In April of 1198, when the first signs of the baroness's pregnancy were observed, Godefroy sent his driver into the village where the matron lived, bearing instructions that she return immediately to the fortress.

Isadora was settled in a room whose walls were hung entirely with curtains, as was required by custom. Edwige, Clémence, Gerlinde, and the wives of the sires' friends were keeping her company, since the birth was to take place only in the presence of women. No man was allowed be present in a home where a woman was giving birth; the baron had to wait outside, as did all the servants.

The matron plunged Isadora into a bath of lavender and chamomile, so that she would relax, and Gerlinde prepared broth for her. She had her squat down onto her bed, supported by the other women. On her right thigh, she was wearing a bracelet of coral, for good luck. The matron sniffed her breath and thought it well; this meant that labor would progress normally.

The baroness showed courage, even though she was suffering; labor lasted a long time, and the child seemed fairly large. Finally, after several hours, she began to feel exhausted. The matron made her drink calming potions, and pressed heavily on her belly. When it was time, she grabbed a large pair of pliers to extract the child. Isadora began screaming; finally, the baby emerged, his head clamped in the forceps. He immediately started crying vigorously.

"It's a boy!" the matron, relieved, cried at last. "What will you call him?"

Isadora could only stammer that it was the godparents' duty to choose their godchild's name.

Edwige, the baby's godmother, replied that—along with the Duke of Sacht, his godfather—they had decided to name him Guillaume. Men with that name had always proven to be courageous and powerful.

All the women congratulated the baroness as she lay, exhausted, on her bed. Gerlinde lit a fire in the fireplace so that her mistress would not take cold. Then, she tenderly wiped her Isadora's brow, speaking softly to her. "Everything will be fine. You have a beautiful baby boy. Just relax; I'll watch over you day and night."

The baby was washed with wine and rubbed down with salt, and then wrapped in linen from head to foot, so as to keep his back straight. The matron recited prayers as she baptized him with oil, praying so that God would greet him in case of death. This corresponded to the baptism, but did not replace it.

When the child was lying in a wicker basket, after having been settled in the nurse's chamber, Godefroy hastened to admire his son. He felt as though he was twenty years younger—the same age as he had been when Quentin and Lidwine came into the world. He was just as pleased and proud at that moment as he

27

had been during that faraway time.

Three weeks later, Lidwine and the Duke of Sacht went over to the castle to congratulate Isadora, who, after a long period of convalescence, was beginning to recover. Arm in arm with Lidwine, she strolled through the garden alongside her friends.

Lidwine could not resist: "Is my father treating you in a sweet and loving manner?"

"Absolutely!" Isadora said; she was quite surprised. "Why did you ask me that?"

"For no reason—or, rather, to make sure that you're happy. But don't worry; I noticed how happy you are when I arrived. It's good to see you like this."

Lidwine, however, could not help thinking of her unhappy mother, who had been martyred by the baron. She absolutely did not want her stepmother to suffer the same fate one day. "Since I know my father well, let me give you some advice: never become interested in another man. He's very jealous."

"Don't worry, dearest Lidwine, I'm not of the sort who seeks the company of a man other than her husband. But you'll forgive me for asking you a question of my own: wouldn't you like for a second child to be born into your household?"

"Oh, yes! That's our greatest desire, and I can entrust safely it to you. I might be pregnant now, in fact, but it hasn't been confirmed. So please, don't talk about what I've just told you, not even to my father."

"I swear I'll be quiet as a mouse. But, if that were true, it would make me very happy."

On the occasion of Guillaume's baptism, the Baron of Lanicey decided to organize a big party in his fortress. He invited all his neighbors and fellow lords; the men were accompanied by their wives. The baptism took place on May 15th, 1198, on a pleasant spring day.

Although she was still tired, Isadora ordered her maids and cooks to prepare a memorable banquet. Edwige and Lidwine participated actively in the preparations. Meanwhile, Godefroy undertook the task of hiring of musicians and troubadours who would entertain the guests between courses.

The baroness brought over a seamstress who would fashion regalia for Edwige and her friends, as well as for Clémence. The latter was breastfeeding her own daughter as well as little Guillaume. Her milk must have been excellent, since the baby took to it after a month. He slept little and opened his eyes often, to his father's delight.

For the festival, trestles supporting large wooden boards were erected in the courtyard; many bouquets of flowers and fruit baskets were placed on it. The sun was not stingy with its brilliance that day.

The guests arrived at last. The ladies, who were richly dressed in embroidered silk, were wearing their finest jewels, which sparkled in the sun. As for the gentlemen, they wore light suits, and they carried their swords for everyone to admire.

On Godefroy's right sat his wife and the highest-ranking nobles in the area. At the sound of the horn, the meal began. It was composed mainly of vegetables and freshly hunted game animals (hare, wild boar and deer either barbequed or baked into delectable pies). The couple ate with their fingers from the same plate, even though spoons and knives existed at the time. Superb wines enlivened the meeting, and the atmosphere soon became very relaxed. The ladies had unbuttoned their clothes slightly, which excited their spouses and friends.

Across from the guests, performing their routines, were highly skilled acrobats, whose limbs were so elastic that they didn't seem to have joints. They seemed tireless, and their pirouettes amused many children. There were also jugglers and fire-eaters, whose antics incited strong emotions among the noblewomen. Meanwhile, the minstrels recited declaimed poems, which they accompanied with music from their lyres. Their songs essentially expressed the pure-hearted courtly love that pretty damsels dreamed of:

"My love my, heart shudders
At the idea that commits
To you for life
And always, tenderly...."

The guests remained seated until dusk. As it was getting cooler, Godefroy suggested that they move into the castle's huge guardroom, which could definitely hold fifty people. This room was the main part of the castle. The furniture had been removed for the celebrations, and only weapons and tapestries adorned the high walls.

Godefroy approached Isadora, Edwige and Clémence, whose beauty he had noticed upon meeting her the first time. At the moment, the young woman was making the acquaintance of a charming, courteous viscount. She asked Edwige who this fine gentleman was.

"That's Viscount Philippe of Noirval."

"Is he single?"

"I think so, but I'm not positive. Do you like him?"

Blushing, Clémence confessed her fondness for him.

"In that case, you'll be able to see him again, because he's coming back from Germany; he was fighting in the war."

"Where does he live?"

"He actually lives in the same county as the Duke of Sacht."

A delighted Clémence managed to sit in near the viscount while they were enjoying the refreshments. Though the door was open, it was quiet outside. Philippe watched her, and then, won over by her grace, he invited her to stroll with him in the castle's park.

It was almost dark; the lighted torches did not illuminate the area sufficiently. The viscount offered his arm to Clémence so that she would not fall. Clémence began fantasizing: would he ask for her hand later on? She secretly hoped that he would.

"May I ask you, my lovely lady, where I may see you again?"

"That won't be difficult, my lord, because I live in this castle."

"Very good! And may I know your name?"

"With pleasure. My name is Clémence of Jaffrerot."

"Are you related to Baroness Lanicey?"

A little confused, she replied that they were friends. It was not really a lie, because Isadora truly liked her.

"I regret that I must leave you now, but I hope to see you again. Thanks for the good company."

"It was a pleasure for me, my lord."

After having bowed deeply to her, Philippe took leave of Clémence.

3

Quentin's Return

Three years later, in 1201, Pope Innocent III appointed Otto IV of Brunswick King of Germany. Philip of Swabia, who had four daughters, proposed that Otto to marry his eldest daughter, though she was only five, but the king refused. Even though Otto IV was elected, the civil war did not end: Philip continued the struggle to regain the power from his rival.

Quentin of Lanicey, who was now twenty-three years old, had fought alongside Otto of Brunswick since 1198. When the latter managed to dethrone Philip of Swabia, Quentin thought he had fought enough to drown his heartache. Aliénor was still alive in his heart, but he finally accepted her death.

However, come three years later, the young man's character had changed: he was confident, and no longer afraid to assert himself. Without intending to, he looked more and more to his father—namely, in that he had become jealous, spiteful, unscrupulous, and ready for revenge. But he lacked the sire's choleric temperament.

One clear summer day, Quentin was galloped up to the fortress of Lanicey on horseback. Recognizing him, the guards allowed him to cross the two drawbridges that enabled access to the main entrance.

Ulric, who had become supervisor of the fortress, hastened to warn the baron of his son's unexpected return.

"What are you talking about?" the baron countered. "Are you sure that Quentin has returned?"

"Lord, I saw him with my own eyes. He's in the guardroom; the servants busy are telling him how happy they are to see him."

"Deuce! Why did he come back so soon?"

"I don't know, Master. I just wanted to warn you."

"Thank you. You may leave now."

Godefroy dropped his quill, as he was trying to make a plan, and began to think. He was deeply resentful of his son; Quentin had acted ungratefully towards his father, and he was too rebellious. Godefroy could not forget his behavior. Thus, he decided to receive him coldly.

When Quentin knocked on the door of his study, Godefroy groaned. "Come in!"

His son had become a very handsome man; he was tall and muscular. His face, however, betrayed a kind of arrogance, as he knew neither his own strength nor his own beauty. The sire was jealous: he no longer had the audacity of youth, which could allow itself to be foolish. However, unlike Quentin, Godefroy had always worshiped his ancestors.

Pointing, he offered his son a chair. "You are not welcome here, and you should know why."

"Actually, no, Father, I know."

"How?" roared the sire. "Did you lose your memory while fighting alongside Othon of Brunswick?"

Quentin made an effort to repent. "Yes, I remember that I didn't follow the path that you plotted for me."

"Is that all? Need I remind you that, three years ago, you fled from here, taking the woman I loved with you?"

In turn, the young man reared up. "Do you call rape love?"

"What do you know about that? Were you there to accuse me of rape at the time? I forbid you! Do you hear me? I forbid you from speaking to me like that. Now, tell me the reason why you came here."

"I came to support you, since I'm tired of waging war. Isn't that enough for you?"

"I'll accept, but on two conditions. The first is that you don't usurp my role as leader of this fortress. Is that clear?"

"I don't intend to. But I hope you'll give my views some thought."

Softening a bit, the sire continued, "Second, if you want to stay with us, you'll have to obey me."

Anger started to take over Quentin, but he managed to control himself. What more could his father want? "I'm listening, Father," he said, sighing.

"I want you to take a wife. It's time for you to settle down."

The young man did not find this inconvenient, since his beloved Aliénor was no longer of this world. His heart had remained free after her death; he had frequented prostitutes during the following three years.

"Who did you choose for me this time?"

"You don't know her. She's the niece of Count Fouchardière. This girl, who's fifteen, is an orphan, and her uncle put her in a convent so that she could complete her education. She won't become a nun, though. In these institutions, most young noble girls learn to read, write, sing, and weave."

But Quentin was not listening to his father's explanations; rather, he was concentrating on one thing. "Is she pretty, at least?"

"According to the count, she's joyful and intelligent. She's also wealthy, being an only child, and her dowry will be generous as well."

Quentin needed only to see a portrait of the girl before giving Godefroy his approval.

"So be it!" the baron said. "I'll speak to my friend, Hugues of Fouchardière. But I'm not going to wait for your approval, since you still need to obey me. You may withdraw to your old apartment now."

Quentin bowed to his father and walked away. Although he'd been acting obedient towards his father, he had always hated him. Meanwhile, the sire was in a good humor; he had managed to impose his will on his son. At the age of forty-five, he had not only dared to remarry with an Alsatian, but the union had also given him a three-year-old son, who he ostensibly preferred. This was quite the inconvenience!

Quentin was anguished to notice how easily the baron had replaced his mother, who had died by his own fault, under despicable circumstances. Moreover, this Isadora seemed so confident here; she commanded the servants with a firm, assertive tone of voice, whereas his mother had been so gentle with them. Finally—even though she was still pretty, despite her thirty-five years—Isadora was less appealing than his mother, before her descent into Hell…. What was it about her that made his father constantly give her presents? As for Karl, her son, he was acting like a confident little lord; at the age of thirteen, he was already full of himself.

All of this was gnawing at Quentin's heart. When he crossed his stepmother on the stairs, or when they ate at the same table, he pretended to ignore her. Then, one day, when they were both standing in the entrance of the fortress and he pretended not to see her, she rebelled against him. "Sire, you should at least say hello, as custom requires."

But the young Baron retorted, "Please know, Madam, that, to me, you're still a stranger. You are not my mother or my friend, and I don't see why I should give you any consideration."

"And all because I'm married to the master of these parts."

Quentin began to chuckle. "Ah! You shouldn't brag so much, Madam, because if you knew what to expect here...."

"What do you mean? What do you mean?" she replied, deeply moved by these shocking words.

The young man understood then that she did not know of the horrible fate that had awaited his mother. For a moment, he felt an intense need to tell her about the atrocities that the sire could invent when he wanted revenge. But he dared not speak a word, for fear that his father would send him back out, should he find out. Instead, Quentin simply replied, "You'll find that out on your own..... I beg you, please don't bother me about it."

And he walked away, toward the stables.

On her way home, her anger having dissipated, Isadora thought about what she had heard. What was Quentin referring to? She could not imagine the baron preparing himself for revenge. And from whom?

As agreed, Godefroy asked the Count of Fouchardière to send him a picture of his niece, in view of her upcoming wedding with Quentin. Next, Godefroy summoned his son to his office at the top of the keep. He held the portrait of Herminie Fouchardière, which had been skilfully designed by a talented artist, out to his son.

The girl was so beautiful that Quentin gaped. "Thank you, Father! If she really does look like the portrait shows, I'll be happy to marry her."

He contemplated the long, thin face, with its soft features

and candid expression, its halo of very long golden hair. Of course, Herminie's beauty could not equal that of Aliénor, but nevertheless Quentin's eyes rested on the mouth he wanted to kiss.

"All in good time!" the baron exclaimed, rubbing his hands together. He was hoping that this young woman could possibly calm his son's youthful passions, and perhaps render him more submissive.

"Ah! If only you knew when I can meet her!" sighed Quentin. "When will the marriage take place?"

"I think that, if everyone agrees, it can be held in a month. I'll go give the good news to my friend."

The servants busied themselves preparing for the wedding, which pleased them greatly, since some of them had known Quentin as a child. Old Hildegarde, also known as 'Hilda,' even wept with joy.

One evening, at night, the old servant slipped out of the castle, over to the small pile of dirt that was Mahaut's tomb, and, all the while shedding tears, she spoke of the recent joyful events. Then, she prayed fervently for Mahaut's soul to rest.

Meanwhile, the young baron gave invitations to some of his former soldiers, alongside whom he had fought in Dijon. His friend Roland Chessac had managed to marry the rich, seductive Aglaé La Rocherie, and their union had given him a son. Quentin invited them to the ceremony, in addition to a senior officer who had taught him the art of archery. This officer was Count Thibaut of Menard, who entertained so many ladies with his charms that he could never bring himself to pick one and, in doing so, risk losing another. Thus, he was free from all attachments.

This is what Quentin wrote to Count Thibaut:

My dear friend and master,

It is my pleasure to announce my wedding to you. It will be celebrated in the chapel of our fortress on September 10th, and I hope that you will do me the honor of attending. My father has remarried; his new wife's virtue seems to be perfect....but I want to make sure. So, if you can come, I'm asking you to seduce her discreetly. I know you're laughing right now. But I know that your charms are irresistible. It would be an excellent test for my stepmother, toward whom, I must admit, I feel some resentment.

I'm hoping to hear back from you soon. Please keep faith in our friendship, and hold onto our wonderful memories.

Quentin Lanicey

As the wedding day approached, the castle's inhabitants found themselves in turmoil. Isadora brought the seamstress back so that she could order new, shiny satin fabrics for herself and her friends. Clémence hoped to see the handsome Viscount Noirval, who was on the guest list, once more; she secretly wished to seduce him. As for Quentin, he longed to see his future wife at last; he would only meet her on the day of the wedding.

The long-awaited day finally arrived. The sun was still hot; it beat down, illuminating the landscape and touching the fortress with red tones.

Herminie appeared, smiling shyly. She was wearing a pale pink satin gown, cinched tightly at the waist, which accentuated her thinness. Her maid had injected lemon juice into her blue eyes to make them brighter. Her translucent forehead was encircled by a long white veil, made of lace, which fell down to her waist. On her veil lay a wreath.

As she was an emotional woman, she was quite moved by the ceremony. When she saw Quentin standing there—stunning in a long black linen tunic, with his hair floating freely on his broad shoulders—she immediately fell madly in love with him. Her face lit up with a radiant smile, and her cheeks turned pink with joy.

Godefroy had ended up accepting that a small religious ceremony be celebrated in the chapel, which was rather too small to hold anyone. Only the parents and the family of the couple could attend. The priest blessed both rings, and then the young couple took their vows.

The inhabitants of the villages adjoining the fortress had been invited to share in their happiness. As they were fond of Quentin, many of them attended the ceremony.

A huge trestle table had been installed outside, behind the sires' tables. It was here where Clémence was fortunate enough to be seated before Viscount Noirval. For a while, she did not dare look at him, so as to hide her distress. She smiled when their eyes finally met. The Viscount asked Clémence about her daughter, who was sitting next to her. "Tell me, Clémence, who is this adorable child sitting next to you?"

Embarrassed, the young woman did not answer right away. Should she tell him the truth? She feared that he wouldn't be interested in her if she did. She preferred honesty, though, so, looking down, she said, "This is my daughter, my lord."

He seemed quite surprised. "I didn't know, Madame, that you were married. Pardon me."

She decided to lie. "Her father left me at birth, so I must raise her on my own."

"On behalf of all gentlemen, that's unacceptable behavior! The Church forbids it."

She sighed. "That was his doing!"

Clémence thought that she would still be respected, and she hoped to once more gain the attention of the handsome Viscount.

But he was already speaking to the neighbor on his left, a beautiful maiden who Clémence did not know. She was dressed somewhat provocatively; her outfit hinted at the swell of her breasts.

The maiden spoke to him. "Are you not a neighbor of our fortress, in the county of Nevers? I believe I've seen you before."

"You're quite correct, my lady. To whom do I have the honor?"

"I'm Adelaide, daughter of the Count of Framonville."

"I'm pleased to meet you. My guess was correct: our parents are indeed neighbors."

Clémence's heart was heavy: she didn't feel strong enough to compete with the young woman, glowing with youth, who was so sure of herself. She would have given anything to regain the freshness of being a young, pretty sixteen-year-old.

Behind the table, the aristocrats had dressed their peasants in their Sunday best. The food was plentiful, and all the guests shared in the newlyweds' joy.

Godefroy was delighted to see this, especially given that his daughter, Lidwine, had told him she was expecting a second child at the end of the year.

After the meal, everyone—with the exception of the villagers—returned to the great guardroom of the castle, where they were entertained by dancers and acrobats. As Baroness Lanicey—resplendent in a long purple dress that highlighted her lovely figure, and whose hair and makeup had been carefully attended to by the faithful Gerlinde—walked among them, she did not go unnoticed. It was at that point that her husband took his leave, as he had been asked outside to deal with a question regarding the festivities, which were to last all night.

Quentin winked at the Count of Menard to invite him to approach Isadora, who was chatting with Edwige Palindrey.

"The bride truly is stunning, do not you think, dear?" Edwige said.

"Absolutely! But she has the youth that we, alas, have lost...."

"Yes, time passes so dreadfully fast these days."

They both stood there, contemplating their lives, and memories of the fifteen past years poured gradually into their minds....

It was at that point that Thibaut bowed deeply before the baroness. "Will you allow me, noble lady, to keep you company? You seem to be the most beautiful lady in this gathering; allow me the pleasure of making your acquaintance."

"It would be my pleasure, sir. You may join us.

"I think it would be better if we were alone, that we may discuss at our leisure."

"But what would you like to talk about?"

"I would like to know your opinion on the events that are currently tearing through our country."

"Pardon me, but I have little interest in politics," Isadora said, but she accepted his request nonetheless. Holding her robe with one hand, she followed the count, who drew away from the crowd of guests, in which his friends had gathered. Thibaut emphatically held Isadora's charming eyes with his own, and she felt a little dizzy.

"Would you care for a cup of wine? It's so hot here; we need to cool off."

"Gladly," she replied, smiling.

He called forth a servant. "Please," he said, "can you serve this lady, since she's very thirsty, and myself as well." Surreptitiously, while the baroness was turning her head to look for her friends, Thibaut poured a small amount of powder into her bowl before raising his own.

"So, I offer this cup to you: you are the queen of all the ladies here today."

"Oh, you flatter me too much! May I know your name? I've never seen you in our county."

"Actually, I'm friends with the Duke of Burgundy. Count Thibaut of Menard, here at your service."

A lovely smile played on the baroness's lips; she was not used to being courted. Godefroy's friends treated her very respectfully. This sire did not know her; he could allow himself to act a bit gallantly around her. But, after a moment, she felt a bit light-headed, as if she had swallowed three cups of wine instead of one. Her head was spinning; she felt as though she would fall down. Pulling her over to him, Thibaut said, "I'm quite fond of you, my beautiful lady! I'd love to walk with you in the garden. The sun is starting to set, and this evening is perfect for romance, don't you think?"

Isadora lifted her head, looking at him with surprise. "You're not comfortable here?"

"I surely am! But it would be more intimate if we took a walk...."

All of a sudden, the spell was broken; Isadora did not want to get any more intimate with the sire, even though he was courteous and quite nice. And, above all, she did not want to act like a woman of loose morals.

"Thank you so very much, Count, but I'm tired. I'd rather rest here."

He took one look at her, disappointed that she had not quite accepted his offer. But no! She had chosen to remain dignified instead.

"That aggrieves me, Madam, but my feelings do not matter. May I keep you company on this sofa instead? Maybe you'd like to cool off again?"

"No, thank you. I only want to rest."

Isadora slumped onto a couch; the Count sat beside her, so

close their legs were touching, and delicately kissed her neck. She shuddered, then rose abruptly, not having appreciated his familiarity. "Know, sir, that I've lost respect for you. Please leave me, I beg of you."

It was then that moment that Godefroy reappeared in the room Seeking his wife, he had no trouble finding her: the purple color of her robe was very noticeable, even from afar. Imagine his surprise at finding her with another gentleman sitting by her side!

The baroness went over to meet her husband. "Ah! You're back at last," she said with relief. "I'm so glad—this gentleman started bothering me after he invited me to drink."

Red with anger, Godefroy walked to the Count of Menard and said, in a tone that did not require a reply, "Sir, whoever you are, I order you to withdraw. I am the master of this place; no one is allowed to bother my wife."

"Very well, Baron. I will take note of that, but I will also inform my friend, the Duke of Burgundy, of what has occurred today."

"Do as you see fit!" he replied. "I'm not intimidated, since the duke is actually a friend of mine. Please leave my fortress!"

So Thibaut walked away; he was in very bad humor. But, before he had finished leaving, he found his friend Quentin, who was with Herminie. Quentin excused himself, and both men went into the next room, where a few old men were dozing in armchairs.

The count told his friend of his mishap. "But," he explained, "everything seemed fine initially. Your stepmother seemed delighted at the prospect of being courted."

"What happened afterward?"

"I thought she would accept a light kiss from me. But instead, she was offended."

Quentin felt his disappointment take over him. "So you weren't able to seduce her! How is that possible? Ordinarily, all the noble ladies are constantly swooning before you."

"This surprises me more than anyone else, believe me—and I'm humiliated, too."

Quentin hastened to reassure him. "Don't worry: you will be avenged. I thank you sincerely for having taken part in this game. Now, please excuse me, but I must return to my bride She doesn't know many people here...and my duty is to stand by his side."

"Of course. But still—keep me posted on this story, should anything more happen."

"I won't forget. Goodbye, my dear friend."

The count left at last.

The priest had blessed the newlyweds' bed so that their union would be fruitful. Quentin undressed Herminie hurriedly and honored her without restraint, even though, as a virgin, she was scared and anxious.

The young man let a few days pass before he went over to pound on the door of his father's study. As he got older, he resembled his father more and more, although he lacked the latter's explosive temperament.

Surprised, Godefroy frowned when he opened the door. "Son, I did not ask you to come here. Do you have a good reason to come bother me?"

"Yes, Father, I have an important reason, and I want you to listen to me."

The lord sighed. "Hurry up, then!"

"Let me tell you. On the day of my wedding, when you left the guardroom where we were all gathered, I caught your wife *in flagrante delicto* with the gallant Count of Menard."

"Well, of course not," the sire corrected him. "She told me he was bothering her."

"That's the version she told you, but it's not the truth."

Godefroy's thick eyebrows, which were shaped like circumflex accents, knit together. "What do you mean by that? What did you see?"

"Well, they both kissed each other—I saw it with my own eyes. Your wife seemed delighted."

The sire remained stunned for a moment, and then he began to think. What incentive did his son have to tell him such things? What could he expect from his son, if not an act of revenge? Well, in any case, he wouldn't believe him. "I'll discuss this with Isadora," he said. "But, regardless, I advise you to mind your own business, not mine. You can go now."

However, that night, he said nothing of it to his wife. Although he was also very fond of her, he also liked her because, as a marquise, she had acquired an education that rendered her worthy to command all the servants and lower-ranked workers. She knew how to make everyone respect her. Further, she was not as jealous as she once had been; time had done its work of appeasement as she grew older.

In November 1201, exactly five years after the birth of Conrad, Lidwine gave birth to an adorable little girl named Lizbeth. To celebrate his daughter's baptism, the Duke of Sacht organized a great celebration at the castle of Vauzelle.

Lidwine knew the immense pain of losing a child; she had lost her own son in October 1198, after he had been born prematurely. The Duke of Sacht had been greatly affected as well; he consoled himself by taking pride in the strength of Conrad, who had been named as his future successor.

Godefroy went to the castle with his family, including Guillaume and Clémence, who was responsible for supervising the child. Quentin found his sister brimming with joy; she knew the circumstances of their mother's death, and this knowledge brought them closer.

"It's too bad my mother couldn't have been with me during the delivery," Lidwine said. "She would have been so happy to help me!"

"That's quite true," Quentin agreed. "I miss her too. And I have to deal with this Alsatian, who's so haughty she thinks herself a queen."

"Do you hate her that much?" the young woman replied, taking offense at his comment. "Did you forget that Isadora's been my friend for a long time?"

"No, and that's what infuriates me. I don't support your friendship."

"Hush, dear brother! I didn't think you were jealous."

Fortunately, the young man had Herminie—whose graces were simply impossible to avoid—to take care of. The latter, having been educated by nuns, read Latin as well as she read French. Her body still resembled that of a teenager who hadn't yet finished growing—a form which accentuated her apparent fragility. Godefroy admired her in silence; he almost considered her as being his daughter. As for Isadora, she was delighted to see her cousin, the Duke of Sacht, and congratulated him warmly on the child, as little Lizbeth promised to be very pretty in future.

"That makes sense," the Duke replied, flattered. "She already looks like my dear wife."

Conrad, however, did not think much of this baby, who spent much of her time crying. He spent much of his time in the garden, aiming the little bow his father had for him in the direction of the trees.

Since the winter season had cast a thick layer of snow on the sleepy landscape, the banquet was held inside the fortress. Othon had hired a troupe of dancers, who were now flowing gracefully around the table, and a troupe of magicians, who were currently entertaining Conrad and Guillaume with their antics. This festival was a success in every respect, and everyone would have happy memories of it—everyone, that is, except for Clémence. It was here that she was counting on running into the seductive Viscount Noirval, even though he was not among the guests. He was, however, becoming friends with the duke; their castles were located in the same county.

Clémence discreetly drew Lidwine to her side, and—after having congratulated her for giving birth to such a beautiful baby—asked her, "May I allow myself to ask you for news of Viscount Noirval? I see that he isn't here today."

"Ah! Dear Clémence, have you fallen prey to his charms? Philippe is famous among the ladies.

Blushing, the young woman defended herself. "Oh, no!"

"Well, I must tell you that he has recently become engaged to the young heiress of a nearby castle."

Clémence could not stop herself from turning pale, but she still had the courage to continue. "And who is she?" Her heart was pounding from shock.

"I don't know if you know her," Lidwine continued. "Her name is Adelaide of Framonville. She's a rich heiress. Her parents' land neighbors that of Philippe's father, so the families often agree to organize marriages between their children."

Clémence was sure she'd seen her before: she remembered the beautiful damsel who the Viscount had been speaing to at Quentin's wedding. She chose to flee in order hide her disappointment. "Please excuse me, my dear, but I need to watch Guillaume. I think he had to leave this room."

4

Dark Days

The civil war was still raging in Germany; Philip of Swabia still hoped to recover the power from his rival, Othon of Brunswick, whose camp had been victorious in 1201.

Following the failure of the Third Crusade—in which Godefroy of Lanicey and the Duke of Sacht participated—Pope Celestine III issued a call to organize a Fourth Crusade in the Holy Land. But the European nobles ignored the call: the Germans were fighting against the Pope, while England and France were at war.

Godefroy encouraged Quentin to participate in the war. "Our kingdom needs young men like you—that is, experts in the handling of weapons, who have undeniable physical strength."

"Perhaps, Father," said Quentin, "but I didn't get married so that I could abandon my wife, as you did with my mother."

"What a heinous thing to say! I forbid you from judging me."

"I'm not thinking anything less. And you can't force me to go; I'm not going to sit back and let you push me to do what you want, like I did before."

The sire glared at Quentin, but he did not lower his eyes. Instead, he contented himself with answering his son. "My son, you are a coward—a coward! It's better to die with honor than to live without glory."

Quentin shrugged, and they remained there.

When one left the Lanicey fortress and headed in the direction of Switzerland, one could admire a landscape that was filled with high rocks and vast coniferous forests. A path cut through the area; on one side lay a forest, and, on the other, a sort of cliff. The cliff was composed of stones; these were very worn, as they had been eroded by the river, which had flowed at the bottom of the valley for millions of years.

In the winter, the roads were still impassable, thanks to the heavy snow that numbed the landscape for several months out of the year. It was so cold that many villagers were died of cold and hunger; they could hardly sustain themselves. As usual, young children and the elderly were affected the most.

In the past, Mahaut had made them distribute their leftovers, as well as fresh blankets, to the villagers. But the new baroness had not had this idea. Godefroy, meanwhile, was not worried about their fate, saying that he had other, more important things on his mind—namely, the future of Germany.

In the castle, the servants could easily light up the fireplaces, as the sire was not lacking in firewood. On the other hand, he also held large reserves of grains, fruit and game, which were procured via agriculture and hunting. Godefroy loved hunting, as did all the sires in the region. He often went hunting during the warm season, accompanied by the Marquis of Attrans and the Viscount of Palindrey; these hunting parties strengthened their friendship.

Everyone was relieved by the arrival of spring, which made the snow disappear and allowed them to travel outside the fortress. Isadora loved riding in the woods alongside Karl, her eldest son. Now fourteen, Karl had frequently ridden horses with his friend Hugues of Chassiniat; he was an excellent horseman. But Hugues, who had finished training with his stepfather to be a page, had regained his family's castle in Lorraine. From now on, Karl would ride with his mother.

One day, the baroness wanted to ride to Switzerland, as she very much liked the steep landscape. Happy to get drunk on the fresh air, her son rode about thirty meters ahead of her. It was late morning, and the day was starting to heat up. Isadora took her time admiring the forest stretching out on her right. The trees were already bedecked with light, tender leaves, and daisies and dandelions brightened the edges of the road. A fairly high cliff, composed of large rocks and covered with shrubs, rose up on her left. Her horse, who was well-trained, obeyed her without any trouble. Suddenly, she heard a low, clear growl moving down the cliff. This unusual noise frightened the horse so much that he reared up, whinnying frantically. Isadora shrieked as she fell, head first, over the horse—and then she lay still. By rearing, the animal had managed to avoid a large stone that had fallen onto the path before them.

Karl, who had also heard the noise, turned around. Seeing his mother lying lifeless on the ground, he cried out. "Mother! Are you hurt?" he said, anguished. "Answer me, please!"

Receiving no answer, he bent down beside her, and noticed a puddle of blood escaping from her head, flooding the ground. But then she moaned weakly; she seemed to be breathing once more.

Karl let out a huge cry of terror. Mounting his horse, he whipped the latter with all his strength so that he would gallop faster. Finally, having arrived at the fortress, he called out to the guards. "Let me pass through! Quickly!"

They obeyed immediately, and stood aside. Karl wanted to warn Godefroy, but the sire was absent. So he searched for Ulric, the overseer of the fortress, and begged him to follow his own horse to the site of accident. Several men escorted him, then tethered their horses at the place where the baroness had fallen.

"Our mistress is dead!" one man, who had approached her first, cried out. "She's not breathing."

"No!" screamed Karl. "That's not possible! She was still breathing when I left."

He grabbed his mother's arms; she was cold, and beginning to stiffen. Her blond hair was covered in blood, and her swollen face was a frightening sight.

Karl, who had become very pale, began sobbing convulsively. Rising, the man carried Karl onto his horse, as the boy felt incapable of walking. Pressing the boy firmly to him, he brought Karl to the fortress.

Knowing that Godefroy had gone to the village, Ulric left to look for him. He found him inside a peasant's house, castigating the man for not being able to pay his taxes. "I warn you, clown, if you cannot pay your due, you will have to work harder!"

The poor man seemed terrified.

Ulric approached the sire. "Master, I have something very important to tell you. Follow me, please." Even as he spoke, the face of the man without a soul remained impenetrable, and his voice did not tremble.

"My God! What the devil could be so important that you came here to bother me?" the sire exclaimed.

"Just follow me, and I'll tell you," Ulric said. It was the first time he had allowed himself to give his sire an order.

Leaving the peasant, Godefroy followed Ulric outside. "So, now can you tell me?"

"Yes, Master." Ulric was speaking calmly, as if he were describing the weather. "Your wife has passed away. Her horse reared in front of a huge stone that broke off the cliff and fell on her head."

For a moment, Godefroy was shocked—and then he roared in anger. "Do you truly believe it was a just an accident?"

"I don't know."

"What did her son Karl say?"

"We can't question him. He's retired to his room, and he refuses to speak to anyone."

Leaving Ulric, the sire mounted his horse and galloped at full speed to the castle. There, he shoved aside everyone in his way, and leaped over to the door of their bedroom. Isadora was lying on his bed, disfigured by the fall. However, a light was emanating from her....

Though his pain was genuine, he did not collapse. Anger outweighed the sorrow; he did not truly believe his wife was the victim of an accident. He thought that someone had wanted her dead, and that that person had thrown launched the stone in front of her horse. Someone who knew she was going to be on the cliff that day—someone close to him, someone who lived in the fortress.

Edwige Palindrey Clémence and Gerlinde took turns watching over the body. As they sat there, looking at their beloved friend and teacher, they recited prayers and shed bitter tears.

No one came to eat dinner that night.

The next day, the priest celebrated mass so that Isadora's soul should rest in peace. She was buried in the chapel, where the sire's ancestors would sleep for eternity.

Quentin did not attend the funeral. He was sickened that his mother had been buried in a remote corner of the garden, in a manner befitting a mere dog, while this stranger was resting with his illustrious ancestors.

For several days, the sire did not show himself; he remained locked up in his office, insisting that no one come disturb him. He tried to force himself not to think, but he couldn't stop himself from reflecting on drama that had left him a widower. He had no doubt that someone had been trying to murder his wife. But why? He thought that perhaps Isadora had been too hard on one of the servants, and that he had wanted revenge..... He could see no other explanation.

A week after the tragedy, he asked to speak to Ulric, his confidant.

Always faithful, the servant walked silently over to him. "What can I do for you, Master?"

"Sit down. This is what I want from you: you're going to speak to all my servants. You're going question them, one by one, in order to find out what they were doing when my wife was out riding. And you'll tell me the names of those who were absent at that time. You'll have Hell to pay if you don't find a suspect!"

As usual, the man without a soul bowed to Godefroy. "You know I'll do whatever you please." His eyes glowed like embers under his thick white eyebrows. Although he was roughly the same age as the sire, he looked older than his master. He began to slump now, and his hideous features seemed to be marked by his crimes.

"You will report to me once you've found the culprit," Godefroy added. "You can leave now."

Ulric went to work; he spoke to everyone—everyone from the servants to the kitchen valets, and not to mention the grooms. Two of them had been on a mission that day, and had left the fortress. But Ulric hated one of them; this peasant did not seem to fear the man without a soul. He was Eudebert Gorgeon, a married father with six children. Ulric designated him as the possible culprit.

Two days later, he went to his master to report his findings.

"So, my good Ulric, do you have any suspicions against some-one?" The sire was nervous; he longed to dispose of this man.

"Yes, sir. It turns out that your servant, Eudebert Gorgeon, was absent from the fortress on the day of the tragedy."

"What was he doing at the time?"

"You had ordered him to go to the cattle fair at Ponthieux."

"That's right, I did," Godefroy confirmed. "I remember now."

"Now, to get to Ponthieux, we must take the path that overlooks the cliff—the one your late wife had ridden around on horse-back."

The sire's eyes narrowed like those of a cat planning to pounce on his prey. "But of course! It must only be that ugly man! Did you know that you're a genius? Ah! Where would I be without you? So, bring me this ruffian tomorrow morning at the latest, and I shall make him confess."

"Very well, Master. I will do as you've asked."

And, with that, Ulric slipped away without a further word. Did he not need to obey his sire?

The next day, Eudebert left the village where he lived with his family, and went to the fortress. The guards, however, would not let him enter.

"Don't go any farther! We've been given orders to stop you."

Eudebert was shocked. "But why?"

"You may not ask questions. We'll take you to the baron."

They seized him, binding his arms behind his back.

The guards pushed a worried Eudebert into a secret room, which was hidden in one of the castle's basements. This room was meant for intimidating or questioning the perpetrators in an area that could be supervised by guards. The poor servant knew that this room was used for torturing men who refused to admit their mistakes. Too horrified to speak, he turned his head around, looking from one instrument of torture to the next. He saw an iron cage of human-sized proportions; this device could be suspended in the air until the crows shredded the man trapped inside to pieces. He also saw a metal collar encircled with quills and tourniquets, as well as chains, which—when heated to extreme temperatures—could be pressed onto soft skin, branding it. He would never have thought that he might one day be pushed into such a collar.

Fortunately, the guards led Eudebert to another room, this one behind the first, where the sire was sitting at a table, waiting for him. He, too, was surrounded by guards.

The baron motioned for Eudebert to sit before him. "Eudebert Gorgeon, if you do not know what you're accused of, allow me to enlighten you!" he shouted. "On the 17th of April, 1202, you knocked a huge stone down the cliff of Quincey, killing my wife! Do you know what I do to murderers? I hang them up in the village square. Your whole family will attend your execution!"

Eudebert shuddered from shock. Despite his trembling, he managed to answer the baron. "No, sir! I would never have dared to do that. Why would I want to kill your wife?"

"Only you would know—and that's what you're going to tell us today."

Standing up abruptly, the servant tried to escape—he couldn't tolerate this longer—but his efforts were to no avail. The guards continued to restrain firmly by the arms.

"Sit back," roared the baron, "and tell us what you did this morning."

"I went to the cattle fair at Ponthieux to get sheep, as you ordered me to."

"Did you take the path that overlooks the cliff of Quincey?"

"Naturally, sir; there's no other way."

"That's consistent with what I remember. What time was it?"

Frightened, Eudebert began stammering. "I don't remember very well.... The sun was already up...."

"That much is true. Did you know that the baroness was walking under the cliff this morning?"

"Of course not!"

The lord pounded the table with a huge fist. "You lie! You're a scoundrel! I'll force you to tell the truth. If you don't, I'll make you spend some time in the room you just passed through."

The servant began trembling once more. His knees clashed together, too fast for him to stop them; his face drained of blood. But still, he found the strength to clear his name.

"I swear I'm telling the truth, on the head of my last child!"

"Shut up! This will be the end of you!"

The guards asked, "Should we proceed with torturing him?"

Godefroy's next sentence melted on his lips as he changed his mind. "Not now, no. Let him spend some time marinating in a dungeon. Maybe that will give him some time to think."

So the guards seized Eudebert and dragged him over to the dungeon reserved for murderers. Thus, he was locked up in the vault where Mahaut had been detained for so long before she had given up the ghost....

For three days, the unfortunate servant rotted in the dark, filthy, damp cellar. The guards brought him only one meal a day, a foul broth in which floated a few dry bread croutons. He still did not understand why he—and not another man—had been accused of the crime. It was true that he had always served his master before, but he couldn't confess to a crime he hadn't committed! He thought of his wife and six children; they must be deeply anxious right now. What would become of them if the sire decided to hang their father?

Leaning against the cold wall of the vault, he felt himself gradually going mad. What should he do?

One day, he dared to ask a guard if he could help him escape. "Have mercy on me! You're of a low rank, just like me. Help me get out of here—I'm innocent!"

But the guard was gruff. "Are you crazy? Besides, if I let you out, you won't be able to so much as cross the drawbridge before they killed you. And they would hang me!"

On the third day of his imprisonment, two guards came to get him; they shackled his hands and feet. He hadn't slept in the vault, and as such he was so exhausted he could barely walk. As they walked together, he noticed, with a thrill of terror, that they were bringing him to the torture room. They tied him up on the table, still in chains, and—despite his cries and pleas that they spare his life—the imperturbable executioner undressed him. Then, he applied a white-hot metal bar to the soles of Eudebert's feet.

The servant gave a dreadful howl. "Mercy! Have pity me! Stop, I beg you!"

"The executioner will only stop if you confess your crime," one of the guards answered.

"But I'm innocent!" he protested again.

Next, the iron bar was applied to his left leg; the smell of burning flesh permeated the room.

"No!" screamed the servant with all his might. "Stop! I'll confess."

"Very well! In that case, we'll get the sire so that he may hear your confession."

Twenty minutes—a period which, to Eudebert, seemed to last centuries—had passed when Baron Lanicey entered the room, tapping the heels of hard leather boots together.

"So, dirty scoundrel, will you tell me your plan now? Is it that you launched a huge stone off the cliffs of Quincey when you saw your mistress and her horse pass below you?"

"Y.... Yes....," he replied weakly.

"And why did you want to kill her? You hated her, did you not?"

"Y.... Yes...."

His voice was barely audible, but the sire was content. "I was sure I would be able to make you confess. And now you're going to pay for it! Yes: I will hang you at the entrance of the village before nightfall tomorrow night."

And with these terrible words—without even bothering to worry about the poor servant—the sire turned on his heel and left the room. "In the meantime, bring him to the dungeon," he ordered his guards.

"Very well, Master," they told him, bowing.

The guards had to carry Eudebert to his vault: his legs were no longer strong enough to support him.

The next day, a gallows was erected in the village. Godefroy had ordered all those who lived on his lands to attend the execution. Eudebert arrived, half-dead, dragged over to the gallows by a carriage. As the executioner tied the rope around his neck, some of the poor spectators prayed that the rope would break, or that the ladder would be too short. If such an event occurred, it would mean that God was granting His mercy, and the condemned person would be pardoned. But such miracles were very rare, and Eudebert did not benefit from one. Instead, the unfortunate man gave up the ghost before his grieving family.

The sire had demanded that all the fortress's inhabitants, and all those who depended on his lands, be present at the execution, so that it might serve as a lesson to them. It also reinforced his authority over them.

The frightened people returned to their humble abodes that night. In their eyes, Eudebert had certainly not committed this crime; he was a serious and dedicated man. But they knew that they, too, could be eliminated for a mere trifle, as the unfortunate servant had been.

After Eudebert's death, Godefroy was finally relived, and he was able to turn the page on his Isadora. He had loved her, it was true, but he had to bow down fate. Instead, he took an interest in the other members of his family. His son Guillaume trotted around behind him, and Godefroy had great pride in the bright, bold child.

Because Guillaume was attached to Clémence Jafferot, the sire opted to keep her in his service, so that she could continue raising the boy. Because he didn't understand why he no longer saw his mother, Guillaume wept and searched everywhere for her. Clémence tried to comfort and entertain him. Fortunately, he got along well with Johanne, Clémence's own daughter, and the two of them played many games together.

The young woman hoped to see the Viscount of Noirval, who had so pleased her at Guillaume's baptism. Indeed, she had secretly fallen in love with him. The noble, handsome knight returned twice to the fortress of Lanicey, but she did not see him: he withdrew to the sire's study to speak with him about domestic politics. He was accompanied by the Duke of Sacht, who deeply lamented his cousin's death. Clémence was greatly pained by this, but she knew that she should remain dignified and inconspicuous. She had no fortune, and thought bitterly to herself that she would never find a husband, especially since she already was a mother.

As for Karl, who was now an orphan with neither father nor mother, the boy was deeply distressed. Wishing to leave the Lanicey fortress, he asked Godefroy for permission to do so.

"Sir, I must admit that, I don't need stay here anymore now that my mother has died. And for that reason, I'd like to leave the fortress."

"But where will you go?"

"I intend to return to Willeim, to our fortress, which is under my uncle's command. I already feel like I can help him, thanks to your lessons."

"It's true that I taught you everything you'd need to know for this kind of responsibility. But you'd still need to continue learning, especially in the military arts."

"You don't need to worry about me. My uncle will pick up where you left off."

Standing, the baron embraced his stepson. "In that case, I understand. You may return to your homeland."

"Thank you very much, sir. I won't forget you."

Karl bowed before leaving the room, but then ran into his room to prepare his pack. He was comforted by the idea of being able to flee this cursed fortress where his mother had been murdered. It seemed to him that, in time, his pain would soften.

Quentin, meanwhile, chose to ignore Guillaume; he was jealous of the child, whose features resembled his mother's much too closely. Instead, the young man spent many days with his sweet Herminie. He was grateful to his father as well.

Isadora's death did not bother him in any way; he had nothing but disdain for her. He was yet more relieved that he could no longer run into her. In addition, shortly before the accident, Herminie had told him that she was definitely pregnant; she suffered from frequent bouts of nausea, and was often tired. Quentin was delighted; he was very fond of her. That love did not resemble what he had once felt for Aliénor; she had literally bewitched him with her divine beauty, and he had loved her with an incredible passion. Unfortunately, she had been murdered, and her murderer's identity had never been discovered.... Aliénor would always be in his heart, but he loved his young wife deeply. Herminie had brought a kind of balance to his life; she had managed to calm his rebellious temperament. Moreover, the young woman was kind and graceful, and she admired him endlessly.... She loved him very much.

Godefroy took it upon himself to call for the matron who had looked after Isadora during her pregnancy, and who had assisted in her delivery. Although she was already more than fifty years old, she was very competent, and had an excellent reputation.

Upon arrival, the matron once more crossed over the fortress's drawbridge, after which point she met with Godefroy. She was glad to see Guillaume, who delighted her with his liveliness and good health.

She was brought to Herminie, who was waiting quietly in her room. Bidding Herminie to lie down, the matron felt her breasts and belly. According to the young woman, her pregnancy had begun earlier this year, and she was due to give birth in the fall. However, when the old woman examined her again, carefully moving her hands over her body, she nodded and said, "I think, noble lady, that you must be mistaken about the date of conception; you're too big to only be in the fourth month of pregnancy. I think you're already in your sixth month, which would explain why you're so tired."

The young woman was astonished. "Oh, no! That's impossible, Ma'am".

The matron thought for a moment, then hesitated before saying, "Unless you were expecting twins...."

"Oh, no!" Herminie repeated, distraught. "I hope you're wrong. All the ladies I know who were expecting twins died!"

"I ask only that you believe me. In the meantime, I advise to you stay in bed most of the time, and especially that you don't wear anything. Eat often, but in small amounts, and drink red wine from time to time. You must eliminate salt from your diet, and protect yourself from the sun."

"Understood! I'll do everything you tell me. But what should I do to avoid the curse? I'm so worried!"

"Wear amulets. They will protect you."

Quentin noticed his wife's worried expression when Herminie and the midwife left the room together. "Is everything all right?"

"I would hope so, sir, but I must warn you that she might be expecting twins."

Quentin had the same reaction as his wife. "My God! Hopefully this pregnancy will not condemn her to a premature death...."

"I pray every day for her," said the matron. "That's all I can do in this case. And if I may say so, I would advise you to do the same."

Quentin was not particularly pious, but he promised to pray for her regardless. A carriage driver picked up the matron, leaving the young man's emotions in disarray. He knew that he would be afraid from now on, but he decided to hide his feelings when he was with Herminie.

"Rest assured, my dear," he said when he accompanied her during her garden strolls. "I pray to the Virgin every day. I asked the priest to prepare a Sainte Marguerite's midwifery bag, so you'll be well protected."

Herminie looked at him with love and trust—which only compounded his discomfort.

The summer was particularly hot in 1202, and the young woman spent most of it confined within the fortress's thick walls. Inside, a very comfortable temperature was maintained. Clémence had befriended Herminie, and often kept her company when she wasn't busy watching Guillaume and Johanne. Together, they would embroider or play checkers, which allowed Herminie to deal with her latent anxiety. They were sometimes joined by Edwige of Jaffrerot.

The Viscountess was rewarded for her prayers and offerings to the Virgin: shortly after Christmas, she finally gave birth to a boy, so the Jaffrerot name was no longer at risk of being transferred a future spouse of one of the family's daughters, once they were old enough to marry.

Meanwhile, Godefroy and Quentin devoted themselves to hunting in the company of the sire's friends: the Viscount of Palindrey, the Marquis of Attrans, and the Count of Fouchardière. They rode into the many forests that surrounded the fortress of Lanicey, where they bid their horses to gallop after the deer and the wild boar. In the evenings, when they returned to their homes, they were very happy. Only the priest disapproved of their hunting, which he found distanced the noblemen from their divine offices. In contrast, the men viewed hunting as a great way of training their bodies for war.

When the peasants had finished harvesting the fruits and grains, and August was in full swing, Godefroy organized—as he did ever year—a party to which all the peasants and villagers who worked on his lands were invited. Another party was scheduled for October, at the end of the harvest season.

He missed having Isadora around; it was she who had known how to prepare for the party, and who had done so for several years. She had taken care to find entertainment for both the young and the old—dancers, acrobats, minstrels, peddlers, and others. In addition, traders took the opportunity to sell their fabrics, as well as all kinds of objects of interest, to the partygoers.

The celebrations were so successful that many lords attended them.

Herminie didn't attend the festival that year, as she was about to give birth. Quentin appeared only briefly at the celebration, as he was concerned about the health of his young wife.

Indeed, a few days later, she screamed out from the pain of her first contractions.

The sire immediately left to go find the matron who had examined the young woman three months prior. As the matron was expecting the birth to be difficult, she had a younger matron—who she was training in this complex art—assist her during the birth.

The maids had prepared a relaxing bath for the young woman. Upon bathing in it, Herminie felt some of her pain subside, and thus regained her confidence. All the men, including Quentin and his father, had been sent out of the fortress. Inside, the female servants, friends and relatives of the new mother rushed over to comfort her; they surrounded her bedside. This was women's business.

But the old matron simply shoved them aside. "Help me to settle her in bed. You can support her by holding her behind the shoulders."

She sniffed Herminie's breath. It was bad, which meant that childbirth would be long and difficult.

As time passed, Herminie suffered more and more; her breathing became panting. She was still wearing the St. Marguerite's midwifery bag, as well as the coral thigh bracelet that would improve her fortunes. She prayed between her contractions; the women around her began to pray as well.

But, after several hours of excruciating pain, the young woman began to cry. "I can't do this anymore! I'm exhausted. Deliver the children now, I beg you!"

"Come now—calm yourself!" the matron repeated every time Herminie spoke these words. "I can't work properly if you don't."

"Why is this so hard? I'm too tired...."

"Because you're expecting twins! I'm sure of it now."

"Oh, heavens! I'm dying! I don't want to die.... Do something to free me from my pain."

"What do you want me to do? You know that the Church forbids me from performing a caesarean on a living woman...."

"Yes, I know. I would have to be dead.... But I want to live! I want to *live*! Do you hear me?"

She felt feverish and desperate; she could not stop crying. Her whole body was dripping with sweat, and her hair was plastered to her face. "I'm thirsty! I'm so thirsty!"

"We're not allowed to give you water," replied the unyielding matron. She looked, for a moment, at this poor young woman, condemned to die before delivering her child. *What a shame!* she thought. *She's little more than a child herself.*

Then she grabbed the forceps—that is to say, a long set of pliers that she slipped into the young woman's body—and pulled with all her might. But her actions were in vain: Herminie's pelvis was too narrow.

Herminie screamed so hard that she then fell back, lifeless, onto the bed. Then, her breathing became labored, as though she couldn't manage to fill her lungs with air. In one breath, she called out, "Quentin....! Help....! Quen...."

Then her face finally relaxed, and her head nodded left, then right, one last time: she was dead.

All the women wept. Only the old matron, who was used to seeing women die in childbirth, seemed unfazed. She had to act very quickly to try to save the life of at least one child. Grabbing a sharp knife, she opened the bowels of the dead young woman. With her fingers, she pulled out a fairly large baby—and then another, smaller child—but the two small bodies did not move....

"I'm sorry," she said. "God did not wish for them to be alive. We must accept His decision."

When the men returned at last, Quentin ran to the room where Herminie had been due to give birth—and found his wife dead instead. Her beautiful face seemed lost in an invisible way.... Waving his fist at the sky, he let out a howl of rebellion. "Lord God, why did you take her from me? I'll stop believing in you from now on."

Then, he went to take refuge in his room. He wept bitterly, but, deep within himself, a little voice told him, *This is only natural. After all, I did cause my mother's death.*

5

Clémence of Jaffrerot

After the death of Herminie, who was buried alongside Isadora in the fortress's chapel, Quentin was despondent for a while. In time, he made an important decision.

Quentin walked into the sire's workroom. The latter had plunged himself into his work, which for him was a way to forget his troubles.

"Enter!" the baron cried when he heard his son knocking. He still did not appreciate being disturbed while he was working, but he relented when he saw his son enter the room. "To what do I owe the honor of your visit?" he said.

Quentin did not answer right away. He took the time to look at his father, as if he would never see him again. The sire had not lost his lustre, despite the tragedies that had stricken his family. His face, furrowed by only a few wrinkles, barely betrayed his age, but the wrinkles did not disfigure his features. His gray eyes still pierced into Quentin's eyes, as if to read his son's thoughts.

"Father, I have come to you to announce my intention of fighting alongside King Otto IV."

"Why do you need to go fight with him? You know I prefer Philip of Swabia. And I hope that, one day, we'll be able to supplant Otto."

"Why? The wars only create unnecessary costs for the kingdom, which is already in deficit."

But the sire persisted in his effort to convince his son. "Philip should be recognized as the sole successor of Henry VI, because Henry was his brother. And before he died, Henry appointed Philip to succeed him!"

"That's not what I'm referring to. I want to reinstate the army because the Fourth Crusade is being prepared in the Holy Land, and I want to feel useful."

The sire got up to congratulate his son. "Oh," he said, "that makes me so happy. So you'll take my estate in this fight against the heathen. You already know that you'll be serving a noble cause!"

"Yes, Father, and I hope that this time we will win. We must have our revenge."

"Well spoken! I want you to crush those heretics, too. When will you leave?"

"I think everything has now been organized. But our king won't join us. Instead, we'll be led by Marquis Boniface of Montferrat, who's in Venice right now. I'll join him there."

"I'm so proud of you! Make a good name for yourself, and prove to them that you're worthy of the barony of Lanicey."

"Very well, Father. In three days, I'll come bid you farewell. For now, I must prepare for the trip."

Godefroy didn't try to keep him; he had never really forgiven his son for his former insubordination. And these days, little Guillaume was enough to make him happy.

The Fourth Crusade set out from Venice. Its real purpose was not to deliver Jerusalem from the grip of the heretics, but to negotiate a contract of carriage with Egypt, whose lands were rich and fertile. Boniface III, the Marquis of Montferrat, was the leader of the Crusade. He himself had trained many of the volunteers coming in from the West.

After Quentin's departure, the sire again felt loneliness weigh down on him. He no longer had the heart to organize celebrations at the fortress. Instead, when the weather was gloomy, he most often he went to see his friends so that he could distract himself by playing chess. And when the weather was good, they all left to hunt in the forest, where the natural world awaited them. His friends, however, were no longer enough for him. He missed having a woman at his side. He had spent a lot of time with Isadora, and she had made him feel masculine. He no longer wished to remarry, but he did enjoy the benefits of having a mistress. Thus, among his circle of friends, no lady could be free from his charms—unless, of course, they were widows and elderly women. He much preferred younger flesh—that, and, naturally, someone who would be faithful.

One day, while dining with Guillaume and Clémence, he gazed into the latter's blue eyes with his own metallic gaze, and noticed that she was blushing. *Well!* he thought. *How did I not notice that Clémence is so beautiful?* Indeed, the young woman's complexion was still fresh, though she was now almost thirty, and she still filled her bodice out nicely. That was all that interested Godefroy. Furthermore, being of noble origin, Clémence had an excellent education. But as she was not wealthy, and had already succumbed to the sin of the flesh, no gentlemen had tried to marry her. And the poor young woman, who was of a romantic character, despaired at the possibility of never knowing love.

For Godefroy, she was the ideal prey. He did not hesitate to take action. One evening, when they were both using the staircase that led to their respective rooms, the sire pinned her against the wall. Without warning, he pressed his sensual lips against her mouth. At first distraught, the young woman screamed and struggled. But Godefroy said, "Come now, Clémence, let it be. I feel your breasts throbbing through your dress; I'm terribly excited. Wouldn't you like to abandon yourself to love?"

As the sire was her employer, Clémence dared not refuse. And so, with a feverish movement, Godefroy undid the fastenings of her his clothes and pulled out her breasts. These were rather large, despite her very slim waist, and he was overjoyed. Feeling his blood boil with desire, he kissed Clémence passionately; she squirmed under his bites. Leading her to his room, he rapidly undressed her—and was not disappointed to discover her milky, curvaceous body.

But she exclaimed, "My lord, the Church won't let us take our clothes off!"

"I have no need of the Church and its priests! I want to enjoy the pleasures of life with you, lovely lady!

Clémence felt pride at these words; she had never heard them applied to her before. She had not for a moment entertained the thought that she could attract a man like her master. His ardor pleased her, and he did not need to open her thighs....

She fell into a deep sleep, leaving her beautiful naked body languid on his bed. When she awoke the next day, at dawn, she found that her terrible lover had left.

Clémence felt both regret and relief. Everything had happened so suddenly the day before! Had she not dreamed up the entire thing? And how should she act when he was around? She thought of confiding in a friend, but she rejected the idea for fear of being misjudged. Edwige of Palindrey was a submissive wife; she had a rigid way of thinking, and would not have understood Clémence's plight. She could not talk to one of the maids, either: sooner or later her tongue would have loosened up, and Clémence hated gossip.

The next day, much to Clémence's surprise, Godefroy behaved as if nothing had happened between them. However, the image of the sire—the sire who had almost torn her dress in trying to grab her breasts, who had pressed his mouth to hers, who was so forceful that she had not dared defend herself as he pleasured her body—followed her relentlessly throughout the day. It seemed to her that her lips still bore the mark of his devouring mouth.

Clémence believed that he had simply succumbed to a moment of weakness. He could not be interested in her; she wasn't important enough for him. But she was mistaken: in the evening, when the girl was undressing for bed, the baron came into her room without knocking. "My dear Clémence! It seems like I've arrived just in time to admire your tempting body. Since no gentleman has requested your hand, and you're living under my roof, it's my right to enjoy your body..."

She searched for a shirt to cover herself, but didn't have time to seize one: the sire was already laying her on the bed, devouring her with passionate kisses. She tried to get away, but this only increased his manly desire for her. She dared not scream too loud, lest she be heard by the servants whose rooms were on the same floor.

It was in this way that Godefroy took her intimacy. When he was done, he fell asleep on top of her. The baron had not uttered a single word while using her body; she had the strange impression that she was an object to him. This saddened her sensitive, romantic heart.

As she was not able to sleep, Clémence decided to get up. But every time she tried to escape, he growled and tightened his grip on her.

When at last the sun appeared, bringing a slight glow into the room, the baron awoke. Clémence pretended to be asleep, but to no avail. Godefroy, who was feeling quite refreshed, said, "That was quite nice, wasn't it? I hope that you'll let me share your bed every night."

The young woman was distraught. "My lord, is that really reasonable? You know that Lent is coming, and during that time the Church prohibits any sexual activity for forty days."

"To Hell with religion! God created us as man and woman. We should make the most of it!"

"Forgive me, but I'm going to have a lot of trouble disobeying the Church's orders like that."

"That may be, but don't forget: you have no choice but to obey me."

And, with that, he dressed and left the room, whistling as he walked.

After careful consideration, Clémence decided to go and confess her sin to the priest of the fortress. This priest was a former Cistercian monk who had wanted to make himself useful to everyone. The baron brought him within the fortress walls so that he could work in the fortress, as well as in the villages that depended on its lands. Godefroy's duty, as leader of the fief, was to make a priest available to his family and his subordinates.

The former monk had been preaching and carrying out confessions in the chapel of Lanicey for twenty years now, and he knew the sire perfectly well. When he had arrived, the priest had noticed that his sire's impiety, and had tried to guide him toward religion. "Sir, I'm very flattered to be in your service, but I see that you don't attend my religious functions. I'm very surprised."

"To be honest, I must confess that I only believe in God only when it suits me. Otherwise, I don't have time to waste on prayers that might prove to be unnecessary."

The priest was so offended that he jumped up. "What? You dare question God's existence?"

"So far, I haven't witnessed any proof that He exists...."

"So what do you make of Bible and the Scriptures? They're sacred texts."

"They might be stories which were made up to make us submit to any law. Effective laws are necessary so that men can properly govern their own societies. As the leader of a fief, I know about these things."

The good priest remained speechless. "Ah! My lord, I must to pray a lot for you, so that divine grace touches you."

"You may pray for me, but don't expect me to change my mind. I believe what I see, and God has never shown Himself to me...."

Seeing that he was dealing with a strong-willed interlocutor, the priest did not insist.

He had been much happier with Mahaut's behavior; she had been devout, and had respected Church law. She had attended the Mass he celebrated in the chapel every Sunday, and had regularly attended confession, even though she had few sins to confess. He had appreciated her gentleness, her manners, and the generosity she showed to the poor who she rescued, without the baron's knowledge, in times of famine.

He had tried to pardon her when Godefroy had imprisoned her in this horrible dungeon for something she had done for purely innocence purposes. But the baron had remained inflexible.

Later, when Quentin had fled with Aliénor, the priest had sought to calm the sire's anger toward his son. But, alas, his efforts had been in vain. He had understood Quentin's point of view, all the while condemning him for quarrelling with his father.

Isadora, too, had proven to be pious, and had always honored her husband, as the Church advised every married woman. Indeed, only the sire resisted his efforts.

One day, Clémence saw the priest reading his breviary in the garden of the fortress. Deciding that she would join him, she looked around to make sure that no one could see her. It was late morning at the time. The maids were busy cleaning the fortress; the cooks were preparing lunch; everyone, in fact, seemed to be occupied. As for the baron, he had gone to his lands to see if his peasants were had been tending to the first plowing. In addition, Clémence had entrusted her children to Gerlinde, who had become her friend.

Clémence approached the priest, her heart beating wildly in her chest. "Father, I would like to talk to you. Can we enter the chapel? It would make me feel safer."

"With pleasure. But what have you got to hide?"

"Come with me, and I'll tell you."

Entering the chapel, they seated themselves on a pew. The young woman felt peace overtake her, and felt that God was supporting her in her confession.

"Have you something to confess?" the priest said, upon seeing her distraught expression.

She looked down, making an affirmative gesture with one hand. "Yes. Admitting this is very painful for me, since I don't like being slandered or feeling guilty. And above all, please don't tell anyone else what I'm about to say."

"Naturally, my child. I'm listening."

So Clémence explained what the sire had done to her, without specifying those details that she considered too intimate.

The priest was silent for a moment, then asked, "I hope that you didn't enjoy yourself."

"Oh, no, Father! Surely not," she added, blushing. "I know that the Church forbids it, and that's why I've come to you."

"My child, I commend you for having the courage to open up to me. But you can imagine why, now, I strongly advise you to avoid all contact with the baron. Otherwise, you'd be living in a state of mortal sin."

"Ah, but how can I do that? He ordered me to obey him. He's my master; he hired me to raise his son."

"Pray to God with all your heart, and He will help you. I'll pray as well, so that you may find the strength to resist him."

Clémence was disappointed by his response. Then it occurred to her: what could she expect from a priest, if not prayers?

The priest added, "If you can't find the strength to resist him, then you may join a convent instead. You'd be completely safe there. I know many noblewomen who have chosen that life."

"But I have to raise my daughter! I don't want to abandon her under any circumstances." The possibility of living in a convent didn't seem feasible to Clémence, especially since she didn't feel particularly drawn to the religious life.

"I'm sorry," said the priest, "but I don't know of any other solution."

"Good. I'll think about all of this. And thank you for listening to me."

After their conversation, the young woman returned to care for the children in the fortress; fortunately, the sire had not yet returned. But in the evening, he went, as usual, to Clémence's room. She was already in bed; she hid under the blanket.

"What's happening, my sweet? Are you ill?" he asked, annoyed.

"No, sir. But I wish to be abstinent during Lent, as I told you before."

"Stop it with the bigotry! You're annoying me!"

76

The young woman still wasn't responding, and Godefroy's anger took over. "If keep on refusing me, I'll just go see a whore. She would welcome me with open arms."

With that, he made a show of leaving.

Clémence rose immediately to hold him back. "Oh, no, my lord! Don't go: I am yours."

Although he had not let it show during their meeting, the good priest was shaken by Clémence's confession. He prayed for her, asking God to blow an idea into his mind so that he could help the young, helpless sinner.

The next morning, upon awakening, he thought he had found the answer. He dressed hurriedly; he knew that the sire got up early to enjoy a moment of solitude. Indeed, the latter was still swallowing a bowl of hot milk—as it was March, it was still quite cold—when the priest came to him.

"Oh! Oh!" he exclaimed. "Why are you visiting me so early in the morning?"

"Forgive me, my lord, for bothering you here, but I'd like to talk to you face to face."

"What the deuce? What do you have to tell me that's such a secret?"

The priest did not know how to go about it. While the baron's actions were very intense, how he would react at any given time remained unpredictable. Nevertheless, he said, "Well, it's been almost a year since your late wife left us, God rest her soul, and I think it would be good if you were to remarry."

"Confound it! I hate it when others meddle in my personal life! Don't you know that already?" And he struck his fist upon the table.

The priest continued regardless. "Let me emphasize, sir: as it was said in the Scriptures, 'it is not good for the man to be alone.'"

"So what? Aren't you alone as well?"

"No: God is with me."

"But that's nonsense! But as for your request—let me reply that, after having been married twice, I need time to rest."

The priest stopped insisting, as he knew how stubborn his sire was. Once he had returned to his room—which was furnished very sparsely—the former monk knelt on the ground and prayed fervently for God to try to save Clémence's damned soul.

However, their conversation had not entirely been in vain; Godefroy gave some thought to what the priest had said. As the leader of a fief, it was important for him to be married. Marriage could strengthen his authority vis-à-vis foreign lords, and give them a reason to consider him. Some of his friends had been married three or four times, as their wives had died in childbirth.

That was why, in the afternoon, he summoned Ulric, his confidant and accomplice in infamy, to his cabinet. He was not afraid to admit his vilest thoughts to the man without a soul. Ulric had never disappointed his master, and Godefroy considered him as a double of himself, albeit one on a lower level.

Godefroy rang a bell to call forth a servant; one appeared immediately.

"Firmin, get Ulric and bring him to me."

"Very well, sir."

Firmin returned half an hour later, now accompanied by Ulric.

"Hello, Master," the latter said in a venomous tone. "Did you need me?"

"Of course! Sit down. You know everything about me; I need your advice."

Ulric waited for the baron's orders without saying a single word.

The latter did not even notice the shadow of recognition that passed over the overseer's malevolent gaze. "Ulric, listen to me. The good priest—whose masses you don't frequent, fortunately—just suggested I take a wife. I think this could assert my power over the foreign lords in our county. What do you think?"

"I don't disagree."

"Good! So, in that case, I thought of Clémence of Jaffrerot. Everyone here knows her, Guillaume loves her, and she comes from aristocratic stock. She also has many talents."

Ulric could not help smiling discreetly. "I know what talents you're referring to, sir...."

Godefroy jumped up in shock. "How so? What do you mean?"

"Master, I don't mean to offend you, but everyone here knows about your connection with her. But I'm not judging you."

"Clémence spoke of it?" Godefroy roared. "Tell me the truth!"

"No, she said nothing. But there were eavesdroppers—eavesdroppers, and prying eyes."

The baron was not really surprised. "Well, if we do get married, then the gossip would stop."

"Naturally, yes. But are you sure that Lady Jaffrerot would be an ideal wife for you?"

"Can anyone really know that? She certainly pleases me," replied the sire.

"Is that all you wanted?"

"Finally! Where do you come into the plan?"

A wild gleam sparkled in Ulric's eyes; it stemmed from the joy he felt at manipulating his master, even though the latter was still his leader. Then, the man without a soul clarified: "If, like me, you frequent the gambling house known as 'The Right Neck,' you might find a person who resembles Aliénor. She looks so much like her that it's as if the Devil has revived her!"

"No! I don't believe you. No woman can be as beautiful as she was…. Aliénor was unique."

"Just go to the pub and see for yourself."

"Oh, my! If what you say is true, I'll go to the pub tomorrow."

The next evening, Clémence waited for the sire in her clean, tidy room. As usual, she was wearing perfume, and had allowed her long, wavy hair to tumble down her back. But this time, he did not come. This saddened her; she had finally found approval in his rough company. Her tender, romantic heart was attached to him. And the young woman, who was now feeling desired and perhaps appreciated, had blossomed over time. Her blue eyes glowed luminously, and she wore clothing with the most daring necklines. Gerlinde regarded her as well as she had Isadora. As for Guillaume, he loved her as he did his own mother, of whom he had had only a few memories.

The priest had noticed Clémence's change in demeanour, but he was the only one who disapproved of it. He said nothing, though; he understood that the young woman had chosen to live in the sin. He hoped to see her confess, but clearly she no longer felt the need to do so.

The young woman greatly feared becoming pregnant and giving birth. As such, she swallowed abortifacient potions, composed of a mixture of fern seeds, ginger and willow leaves.

Clémence waited for the sire for several hours, during which time she listened to every noise, in the hope of hearing the sound his boots. Then, despite her anxiety, she fell asleep. Her bed seemed too big for her, and she did not sleep restfully.

When she went down to the kitchen the next morning, her face was crumpled. Gerlinde was already getting ready to serve her.

"Do you know where the sire was last night?" Clémence asked her maid.

"No. Wasn't he with you?"

Clémence had no choice but to sadly admit that she had not heard him return.

"Maybe he returned late at night, and preferred not to wake you up?"

"If only that were the truth!" She swallowed her bowl of milk, though she had no appetite.

Half an hour later, Godefroy appeared in the kitchen. Unlike Clémence, he seemed to be in a rather good mood. What had he been doing the night before? But Clémence did not dare ask him; she knew that doing so would have bothered him. He was back, after all. Wasn't that the important thing?

The night before, Godefroy had accompanied Ulric to the gambling hall known as The Right Neck, which was located at the edge of his territory, beside the canton of Vaud. He hadn't been there in a long time.

The landlord greeted him with a very low bow, then bade him sit at the best table. "What can I serve you tonight, my lord?"

"A pitcher of your best wine."

While waiting to be served, Godefroy considered the customers who were drinking and laughing loudly. Having completed a day's hard work, many of the peasants and artisans were enjoying themselves before returning home to their wives. Most of the patrons, however, were miserable; they were content to converse among themselves, sometimes without even consuming alcohol. Traders, as well as the wealthiest travelers, allowed themselves to follow the brazen waitresses to the back room. There, they lavished the men with their special favors. These prostitutes were often young orphaned women without families, or poor girls who had been rejected by society after they had been raped.

Ulric spotted a beautiful young woman that all the men were

asking for—and who, as a result, earned a lot of money for her boss. Turning to his master, he pointed her out to him. "Look closely at the brunette over there, and tell me you don't see Aliénor in her features."

"My God, they're almost identical! I'll invite her to our table. Ulric, go fetch her for me."

Ulric ordered the young woman to go to the sire's table. Not the least bit intimidated, she asked, "Will he pay me dearly?"

"If you'll seduce him, my dear, I have no doubt of it." And he pinched her buttocks.

She followed Ulric to the table where the baron was sitting. "Sit down," he said, devouring her with his eyes. "What's your name?"

"Tiphaine."

"And your last name?"

"I don't have one. I was abandoned at birth and grew up in an orphanage. When I was thirteen, I was so unhappy that I fled. A man found me begging in a village, and he brought me here. Now the landlord of The Right Neck sees me as his own daughter."

"Very well! And how old are you now?"

"I'll be nineteen soon—or, at least, that's what I was told by the priest who came to get me."

A tall, thin, girl, Tiphaine was rather beautiful. Her long black mane matched the color of her eyes, which shined like stars in the night sky. Her perky breasts arrogantly stretched over the fabric of her red dress, which was pulled tight around her waist. Her sensual lips, brightened with red makeup, made a deep contrast with her smooth, olive complexion, as did her dark eyes. The sire could not judge how shapely her behind was, as she wore many petticoats layered on top of each other.

Tiphaine boldly watched the sire, certain that she was pleasing him. She was bending in such a way that he was overcome by the breasts showing from underneath her dress, which had holes cut into it. She wore an enchanting fragrance as well. Indeed, everything about her reflected a strong sensuality, which Godefroy could not resist.

"Take me into the next room; I want to get to know you better."

She rose, twirling her skirts, and led him into the back room where she worked. After disappearing behind a screen, she reappeared wearing a shiny cape of black silk.

"You can take it off me, sir," she said with a flirtatious smile.

Trembling with lust, Godefroy snatched the cape off her body; Tiphaine was naked underneath. Her buxom body had been shaved, completely and carefully. He passionately kissed her body, and then he undressed. Bidding him to lie down on an old sofa, she leaned toward him, so that the tips of her amazing breasts caressed his stomach; he shivered in joy, and she fell into in his arms. He closed his eyes to better savor this moment...

...and, when he reopened them, she had already disappeared.

"Confound it, am I dreaming," he asked pensively, "or is this girl making me crazy?"

He returned to sit with Ulric, who was drinking as he awaited his master. He had already swallowed two large tankards of wine.

"So, what did you think of the damsel? Was she to your taste?"

"Oh! Thank you very much for bringing me here. She's so beautiful and talented! I'm still in shock."

"Don't you think she's worth as much Aliénor?"

But Godefroy did not share this view. "This little whore is truly superb, but they can't be compared," he said, pouting contemptuously. "Aliénor was a virgin, and she came from an aristocratic family, even though she was gentry. Tiphaine doesn't even know where she comes from!"

83

"Would you come back here?" Ulric asked; he was a little disappointed.

"I will certainly return; this creature has bewitched me. But she can never replace Aliénor."

"So, if you loved her so much, why did you want to get rid of her?"

"Because she refused me—my son had seduced her. So my passion turned into hatred.... She no longer deserved to live."

The lord's face hardened as he reviewed these memories. He had not forgiven Quentin for his arrogance.

After that night, it became customary for Godefroy to attend this infamous establishment; he was tormented by the desire to enjoy himself in Tiphaine's arms. The landlord had made some arrangements to make the room more pleasant. Swathes of brightly colored fabric were stretched over the crumbling walls, and the sofa's canvas had been replaced by velvet. He had also placed two silver candlesticks in the room, so as to illuminate their lovemaking with a soft glow. All of this was thanks to the money that the baron had cheerfully sent his way—since, as a good merchant, he had raised the price of having a tryst.

The landlord had also introduced Godefroy to two pretty girls who delighted his regular customers. But although the sire would have appreciated their skills, he still preferred Tiphaine.

Every in the evening, Clémence waited for the baron for a very long time; she hoped that he would reappear out of the blue. This still happened from time to time, but, alas, it was rather rare nowadays. And when he did come, she got the feeling that his mind was wandering somewhere else.... As she was a submissive partner, she still enjoyed spending time with him, but she did not dare ask him any questions. She had learned county that a woman—even one who had been cheated on—should continue to admire and honor her husband or lover, since women were of lower status than men. Nevertheless, Clémence was suffering internally.

To cope with her feelings, she confided in her friend Gerlinde. "Do you know what our master does, when he leaves at night?"

"How would I know? I'm but a servant."

"Maybe you can find out from a servant who's close to him?"

Gerlinde hesitated for a moment. "In that case, you'd have to talk to the overseer, Ulric. He's the only one who might know everything the sire does. But I won't deny that I dislike him."

"You're not the only one. I think he's deceitful and wicked."

"Hold your tongue, please. You know that the walls have ears."

In the end, it was not necessary to question Ulric: one beautiful summer afternoon, Clémence seated herself underneath an oak tree in the garden of the fortress. She felt that being in contact with nature would recharger her. While resting, she noticed the gardener talking to Ulric. Doubtless Ulric was admonishing him because he hadn't removed the weeds that currently were invading the flowerbeds quickly enough. Indeed, Ulric was responsible for overseeing everyone else's work—that, and to denounce to the sire the names of those who didn't seem busy enough.

It was at that point that Ulric saw Clémence, and he used the moment to go over to talk to her. Approaching her, he arrogantly undressed her with his gaze; the young woman could not help shivering in fear.

"Is this how you're watching over Guillaume?" he said cruelly. "Why isn't he with you?"

"Because he's napping at the moment. Anyway, I have to go inside to check on him soon."

"And who's watching over him while you're relaxing over

here?"

"My servant Gerlinde. We're friends, and sometimes we help each other out."

He began to chuckle wickedly. "Your life is still good right now, but it won't last, believe me."

Frightened, her heart pounding, she asked, "What do you mean by that?"

"Well, you should know that our master is infatuated with a girl who's prettier than you."

Clémence remained speechless from shock; then, she dared to stammer, "How do you know?"

"I know because I often accompany him during his lively evening trips. The girl would tempt a saint if she could."

And he began to chuckle wickedly, enjoying the huge disappointment that registered on Clémence's distorted face. The latter, unable to hear any more, suddenly stood up and—without bothering to say goodbye to the man without a soul—ran off. Once she was back inside the fortress, she told Gerlinde what she had learned. Hot tears soaked her pale cheeks as she spoke.

Genuinely pained for her friend, Gerlinde tried to comfort her. "Come now, my dear. You know Ulric can tell the worst stories you've ever heard! The man is more or less represents the Devil on earth."

"Yes, but I think he was telling the truth this time, since I've noticed that our lord is no longer interested in me. This is such a disgrace! I'm so miserable!"

"What are you planning on doing?"

"I don't know yet, but I won't stand for the servants' gossip. Their tongues will lash out behind my back; I can already hear them gloating."

At that moment, Guillaume woke up, and she left to care for

the child. Doing so was like a balm for her suffering.

It was at that point that she remembered the priest; she decided to meet with him once more. She knew he went to pray in the chapel every evening, so she headed in that direction. The door opened, creaking, as she tried to push it open. The former monk turned around at the noise. Recognizing Clémence, he smiled as he greeted her, then asked her to sit down. The young woman was so moved that she began to cry.

Softly, he asked, "Come now, my child—what's going on?"

"Oh, my Father, if only you knew how much I'm suffering!" And she sobbed harder.

Then Clémence told him what he already knew; word of her affair with the sire had already circulated throughout the castle. Nevertheless, he listened attentively to her speech.

"Madam, you must know that I prayed a lot for you, to beg for the salvation of your soul."

"Thank you very much. Now, I know I want to stop living here; this life is not for me. I thought hard, and I have made my decision. I want to go live in a convent.

"Ah! That is an excellent solution! But about your daughter?"

"I intend for my friend, the Viscountess of Palindrey, to raise her. She'll be in good company, and she will be raised religiously. Edwige can also take her to the convent to visit me."

The priest was delighted. "I am pleased, Madam, that God heard my prayers, for it is He who dictated the right decision to me. Tomorrow, I'll meet with the abbess of Fontenay so that you may be admitted in her abbey."

Sighing, Clémence added, "By leaving here, I'm only worried about one thing: abandoning Guillaume. He's already lost his mother, the poor child!"

"Don't worry about him. His father will quickly find someone to replace you when you leave."

Clémence, a little frightened by all of this, asked, "Will I have to become a nun?"

"No. You can seek refuge there without taking vows."

"In that case, I feel better about my decision. Thank you for the kindness you've shown me."

Clémence got the consent of Edwige Jaffrerot, who assured her that she would raise Johanne with her children. She also agreed to take her to the Abbey regularly, so that she might visit her mother as often as possible.

A month later, after having tightly embraced Gerlinde and the other faithful servants, Clémence slipped out of the fortress without warning. The priest accompanied her in a carriage lent to him by the convent.

6

Quentin's Revenge

In 1202, the Marquis Boniface of Montferrat, Italy led the Fourth Crusade in the Holy Land. The pope had been preaching this Crusade since 1198. But, in contrast to previous Crusades, no king took part in the fourth. King Richard Lionheart of England had passed away. The Pope had prevented King Philip II of France from participating, on account of his divorce. As for Germany, it was torn apart by constant strife between Otto IV of Brunswick and Philip IV of Swabia.

Having left for Jerusalem, the Crusaders—a group composed of about thirty thousand western warriors—deviated from their path to reach Egypt. They were attracted to this rich country for purposes that were purely commercial.

In 1203, the Crusaders took Zara, a Christian town in Dalmatia. There, they met a young prince, Alexios IV, whose father, Isaac II Angelos, had been dethroned. Brother-in-law to Philip of Swabia, Alexis was also the son of the Byzantine emperor. He asked the Crusaders for help; they agreed to assist him, in exchange for a large sum of money and the maintenance of their soldiers. Having become allies, they continued together on the road to the Byzantine Empire. When they arrived at Constantinople, one of the most beautiful cities of the time, the Byzantine emperor fled, taking many treasures with him.

The Crusaders found the Byzantines well-mannered and effeminate. In turn, the Byzantines judged the Crusaders to be coarse and brutal. A civil war broke out between them, and Alexios IV was strangled. Horrified by the murder, the Crusaders captured Constantinople in 1204. Thus, little by little, the Byzantine Empire began to fall....

The Crusaders founded the Latin Empire. The Byzantine Empire became fragmented, owing to the feudal system that was still in force. Boniface of Montferrat became king of Macedonia. Greece, which was part of the Empire at the time, was also partitioned.

The Venetians carved out the lion's share of the land: they got the major ports, most of the islands, and a vast swathe of Constantinople. Most importantly, they gained a profitable commercial franchise throughout the Empire. Thus, the old state of Macedonians—whose organization was already modern, being centuries ahead of the countries in the rest of Europe—was downgraded to having the status of a colonial empire and a feudal kingdom.

Quentin of Lanicey had a chance to shine during the siege of Constantinople, which lasted several months. Having become a master of swordplay thanks to his military training in Dijon, he slaughtered many infidels. Although his shoulder was slightly wounded, he considered himself lucky, he healed quickly. Unfortunately, he lost his valiant companions in the siege. When the Byzantine Empire was dismantled, Boniface of Montferrat rewarded him by letting him govern a piece of land in Cappadocia.

On this land there lived an old aristocrat who had been stripped of his possessions. Quentin visited him on several occasions, and all the more so once he met his daughter, Aysu, who was as beautiful as a rare gem. The old man told him that Aysu, who was his youngest daughter, was not yet married, and that her name meant "moon water".

For the young baron, this girl seemed to have come from the moon. She was a drop from the moon, which he needed to quench his thirst for love.

Aged sixteen, Aysu allied her beauty with a softness that reminded him of Herminie, even though Aysu was very dark and more robust than his late wife. But she was fierce, which further increased his attraction to her. He had to visit much more often before he was finally allowed to speak to her. She had studied French and spoke it very well, according to her father, but Quentin was not able to hear her voice.

Like all women from that area, Aysu wore a long silky tunic over baggy trousers. A belt was cinched around her very thin waist, and her black hair was hidden by a turban. Tall and thin, she resembled a liana.

One day, Quentin gave her flowers with the hope of taming her. Aysu seemed delighted, and she bestowed him with a wonderful smile. And, with that simple gesture, he fell madly in love with her.

He went to her father, who was sitting in the garden, under the shade of a palm tree. "My lord, I know you that your daughter is precious to you, and that she honors you. But she's so beautiful! Would you give me her hand?"

The old man was quite surprised. "Let me think about it. You, the Latins—you're so different from us! You don't have the same customs or the same beliefs as us. Do you believe in God?"

Quentin made an evasive gesture. "Yes, but I'm not a practicing Christian."

"We must believe in Him; it is God who guides us throughout our lives. In these parts, the people have been Orthodox for a long time, as our culture is Greek in origin."

"So what must I do to capture your daughter's heart?"

"You'll need to convert to the Orthodox religion."

"Very well. I'll join this religion."

Quentin was overjoyed. Changing his religion didn't much bother him. Like his father, he had never been very religious; this forced conversion did not bother him.

And so it was that he became an Orthodox Christian for the beautiful Aysu. When he visited girl's father a week later, he welcomed Quentin as his future son. Aysu, he said, had accepted the proposal, and Quentin was overjoyed.

The day of the wedding finally arrived. Because the old man was bankrupt, the ceremony took place in private, and only a few members of his immediate family attended. He owned only his humble home, which was surrounded by a fairly large garden.

Though it was autumn, it was still warm. Aysu wore a long yellow silk dress over her trousers, and a turban of the same color. Quentin gazed at her with adoration.

The Orthodox marriage was not merely a ceremony, but rather one of the seven sacraments of the Church. The ceremony took place as follows: the patriarch (which was the name given to Orthodox priests) asked the engaged couple for their consent. They both agreed to live together and be faithful to each other. Then, it was time for the coronation: Aysu and Quentin each carried a lighted candle, both connected by a single ribbon, and a guest held a crown above each of their heads. The patriarch crowned them as being husband and wife. The patriarch offered them a glass of wine, which they drank together. Finally, holding hands, they walked around the altar three time; they were guided by the priest.

When it was time for them to kiss, Quentin passionately kissed the young woman's plump, sweet lips.

On the wedding night, Quentin was plunged into a voluptuous state of bliss: although she was a virgin, the beautiful Aysu was quite lascivious.

After two long years of waging war in the Middle East, Quentin suddenly felt homesick. Because he didn't live along the coastline, he couldn't bear the sweltering heat of Cappadocia. He was also nostalgic for long winter evenings spent sitting before a good fire, in the company of family.

He asked Aysu for her opinion. "Tell me, my dear, what would you think of living in Germany? It has amazing forests, and the mountains are mesmerizing."

"I would be sad to leave my country, and my father, but I would follow you to the end of the earth if you wanted me to."

"Ah, you're so lovely and sweet!" And he hugged her.

The old lord was saddened by his daughter's departure, but the Gospels made it clear that a wife should follow her spouse. Thus, he made an effort to pretend that it didn't bother him.

The journey was long and arduous, as they came across a violent storm while they were at sea. One night, they heard the wind roaring through the ship's sails; the wind was advancing, moving through the dense fog. The waves turned black and rose up high—high enough to flood the passengers, who screamed in fear. The storm raged so violently that sails were torn and ropes were split into pieces. Realizing how small they were when faced with the enormity of the storm—which, to them, seemed like a divine curse—the passengers feared that they would perish.

Aysu had never traveled by boat before, and she suffered from seasickness. Although she was nestled in her husband's arms, she was first seized with nervous trembling, and then she began to cry. She feared that she would never again see her dear father....

The ship creaked under the onslaught of breaking waves. The sailors tried to straighten the sails, but this was not easy. Quentin thought the ship would start leaking, and tried to hide his concern.

Aysu was on the verge of tears; she prayed to God for the terrible storm to end. "Lord almighty, have mercy on us! Let the sea be calm so that we arrive safely. I believe in Your goodness."

The Divine must have heard this humble prayer, which had sprung from a pure, sincere heart, since—after two days had passed—the sea calmed.

Aysu was stunned when she discovered the forests and hilly landscapes of Germany. But she was even more surprised when she arrived at the fortress of Lanicey. She had never imagined that people could live cloistered inside these high walls; she had been accustomed to wide open spaces in her home country. Fortunately, Quentin had explained their lifestyle to her during their long journey, so she was not afraid.

She had to cross over the enclosure, which was guarded by armed men. Then, when the huge entrance gate opened, she was impressed by the large reception hall, where many people were gathered. Everything seemed huge and cold.

Her husband was greeted by cries of joy: the humble men and women of the fortress bowed fervently to him, welcoming him back home.

Quentin introduced them to Aysu. "Thank you, my good people. This is my second wife, Aysu. You'll have to respect her."

"Good lord!" they chorused, then bowed down low to her.

"Is my father here now?" Quentin asked.

"Yes, sir."

"In that case, tell him that I've returned. Second, please get our belongings settled in my old room." Then he turned to his wife, whose large black eyes were wide open. "My dear Aysu, I must warn you that my father is not as kind and generous as your father is. But you'll get to know him in time."

"I hope so," she replied, feeling a little intimidated.

Everything in this castle seemed inhospitable, if not downright sinister; a shiver ran down her spine. Would she succeed at adapting to its dark atmosphere?

The sire indicated that he wished to see his son in his study. Quentin chose to go without his wife; he feared her responses, as they were which were sometimes too frank. He confided her to old Hildegard, known as 'Hilda,' who was still alive, though she was older than fifty.

"Take care of my wife," he suggested. "She's sensitive from all that disorientation."

"Don't worry, my dear Quentin. I'll take care of her."

The young man left to report to his father, who received him very well. "Ah! You're back? I hope that you have good news for me. Sit down and tell me everything."

Examining his son, Godefroy found him quite handsome: his sun-tanned skin brought out his blue eyes, as well as the blond in his hair. His shoulders had widened, and his muscles were bulging under his clothes.

Quentin, meanwhile, remarked that the sire had not changed since his departure. Indeed, he always looked the same, as if time had no power over him.

Pushing aside the manuscript he was reading, Godefroy listened carefully to his son.

"Father, I have excellent news for you, but perhaps you already know of it?"

"Yes, I heard that you were victorious, and I'm very happy."

"We managed to invade Constantinople, and the Byzantine emperor was forced to flee."

"But," the baron replied, astonished, "I thought you had left to hunt the heretics in Jerusalem. Did you not do that?"

"Boniface of Montferrat changed destinations along the way. He wanted to go to Egypt so that we could develop our trade." Quentin then recounted their adventure with Alexios IV, and their decision to invade the Byzantine Empire to avenge the prince's murder.

"Since the Byzantine emperor had fled, we were able to conquer a large part of this empire, which now belongs to the Crusaders."

"That's wonderful!" the sire exclaimed. "Son, I'm very proud that you fought in this Crusade. You've helped us increase our power in the lands of the Levant." His gray eyes were sparkling with joy. "You may go now. I'll meet you during dinner."

"Er—No, I still have something important to tell you."

Caught off guard, the sire looked suspiciously at him. "What now?"

Quentin had to announce that he had taken a wife there—a task which, to him, seemed much more difficult than describing his military conquests. It was some time before he began speaking. "Father, I must tell you that I got married in Cappadocia." He said all this in one breath, but his eyes had fixed on the sire, and he had stared at him without blinking.

He didn't need to wait long for his father's rage. Red with anger, Godefroy suddenly rose from his chair. "How dare you do this?" he bellowed. "You know that only I can decide who you should marry."

" But," said Quentin," I'm a grown man. I am twenty-six years old, and only I can decide my future."

"You may not!" retorted the baron, whose mustache was

trembling with rage. "Is she a heretic?"

"No, she's Christian, like you and me, and her faith is stronger than ours. Need I remind you that Philip of Swabia—a man for whom you would love to ascend to our country's throne—married a daughter of the Byzantine emperor?"

"No, I haven't forgotten, but he was punished for it: he didn't father a son!"

Quentin continued insisting so that his father would accept his pretty Eastern flower. "Maybe you'll like once you've met her. Should I introduce her to you? She's very beautiful."

"What? You've her brought here?" he yelled. "Quentin, I thought you were rational now, but it seems that you dared oppose me yet again. This is too much, I tell you! Get out from my sight!"

Quentin, who was furious as well, slammed the door shut. He walked around the garden in an effort to calm himself down; he wanted to hide his anger to avoid scaring Aysu. When he reappeared, Aysu was chatting with Hilda as she waited calmly for him. Captivated by her grace and goodness, the former nurse had already taken a shine to her.

Quentin was surprised to see that Clémence wasn't with them. "Tell me, Hilda, do you know where Clémence is? I think she and Aysu will get along very well."

"Ah, my dear Quentin, if only you knew the truth! But I must hold my tongue. I can only tell you that she left us to join a convent."

"Could it be? I remember how she wanted costs to get married at all costs.... So she wasn't able to find a husband who would accept her as a single mother?"

"Well, that didn't end up happening. Clémence sought refuge in a convent instead. Please don't ask me any more about it."

The young man knew that something strange must have happened, but what? "So who's watching Guillaume now?"

"A friend of the Count of Fouchardière—or, rather, a former mistress of his who he wanted to get rid of."

He sneered with laughter. "This child has attended a good school since he was young. Good for him!"

That evening, at dinnertime, Godefroy did not go downstairs to join them. Instead, he ordered a servant to bring his meals to him in his office. Surprised at his behavior, Aysu turned to Quentin. "I haven't yet had the pleasure of being introduced to your father. When will get to I meet him?"

Quentin couldn't stop himself from sighing, but he found the strength to comfort her. "Don't worry, my love. I spoke to him earlier, but he seemed unwell."

"Oh, I see. I hope he recovers quickly."

The young man said nothing; he was trying to think of a solution to their argument. Alas, knowing how stubborn his father was, he didn't expect him to change his mind. They went to bed soon after, but Quentin couldn't sleep. He lay awake in bed, feverishly trying to come with new arguments for his father to accept his new wife.

He stayed awake thinking until dawn was dimly illuminating the room, at which point he realized that the best solution for the moment was to save Aysu, and then hasten away from this sinister fortress. It occurred to him that he should introduce Aysu to his sister Lidwine, who would surely understand his plight, and who, moreover, never afraid to butt heads with the sire. As for the Duke of Sacht, he would probably welcome them, even though he was very friendly with the sire. And who knew? Perhaps Othon would be able to have a positive influence on his former comrade in arms. Relieved by this solution, Quentin finally managed to fall asleep.

He slept very little; a servant woke him up two hours later, notifying him that the baron wanted to talk to him once more. He dressed hurriedly—but very slowly, so as not to wake Aysu—and climbed down the winding stairs that led to the sire's study.

Inside, the sire was already waiting; he was standing his ground. "Quentin, if I've asked you here, it's only so that you may take part in a decision I've taken regarding your affairs. I intend to ask the Pope to annul your marriage."

The young man jumped up in shock at his arrogance. "Why? You don't even know my wife!"

"It doesn't matter why I'm doing this."

Quentin laughed nervously. "Father, that will be impossible; we've already consummated our marriage. The Pope will reject your request."

"We'll see about that! But if he does refuse, I'll compel you to divorce your wife. Instead, you'll marry the eldest daughter of my friend Béatrix Palindrey."

Quentin revolted at these words, crying out with all his might, "Never! You hear me? Never!"

So Godefroy, drunken with rage, got up and threw his chair across the room. Walking toward his son, he seized him by the neck. "If you resist me, I'll go to a lawyer and disinherit you in favor of Guillaume. You won't have a fortune."

"Why would I care for your fortune and your land?" So angry at this injustice that he could feel his hatred taking over him, Quentin added, "Under these conditions, you must understand, Father, that I no longer wish to remain in your castle. The atmosphere has become unsustainable."

"And where will you go?"

"First, I'll introduce my wife to my sister. Then, we'll stay with a friend I know from my military training in Dijon. I'm not going to give you his name."

"All right," replied the baron. "The main thing is that I don't find you here. You've been far too rebellious."

Quentin had to lie to his wife to conceal his father's rejection. He explained that the sire was so ill he could not leave his room. Feeling sorry for him, Aysu agreed to go visit the castle, in the county, where the Duke of Sacht lived with his family. The Duke longed to introduce her to Lidwine, as her husband had often spoken of her in glowing terms.

The fortress's driver drove them there by carriage. The young woman was delighted to discover new landscapes that were so different from those of her native country. The sea was absent, it was true, but she admired the powerful forests that encircled pristine green lakes. Despite her joy, however, autumn was ending, and she was suffering from the cold.

Lidwine welcomed the young couple with open arms. Her brother's absence had weighed her down; she had feared not seeing him again, as so many young warriors had been recruited into the Fourth Crusade. She held embraced Quentin very tightly, then turned to Aysu.

"Lidwine, I'm pleased to introduce you to my bride, Aysu, who's from the Byzantine Empire," Quentin said.

"You're welcome among us. I see that my brother loves you, so you are my sister now. I hope that you're not too tired from the trip."

"Thank you very much, Madam Duchess. I'm very touched by your kindness," Aysu replied, smiling.

"Call me 'Lidwine.' It will be simpler."

At that moment, Conrad and Lizbeth broke into the reception room, laughing joyfully as they played with their toy balls.

Aysu exclaimed, "Oh! Those children are so beautiful!"

"In that case, I hope that you become a mother soon, too."

The Duchess called forth a servant. "Fanchon, can you take my brother and his wife to the room on the first floor?"

"Very well, mistress."

Aysu had not forgotten the austerity of the Lanicey fortress; she felt reassured in the brightly illuminated castle.

When the Duke returned from a hunting trip, overjoyed at having killed a deer, he welcomed Quentin's new wife with open arms, even though she was foreign. He gallantly kissed her hand and said, with his most charming smile, "You're like a ray of Mediterranean sunshine, my dear Baroness; it rains a lot in our region."

"I'm very happy to be here," said Aysu.

"Make yourself comfortable. If you get cold, a servant can light the fireplace in your room."

Until the beginning of 1204, Quentin and his wife had an excellent time at Castle Vauzelle.

When it wasn't too cold out, the two women went to walk to the next village, accompanied by the children. Otherwise, they sat by the fireplace, chatting as they embroidered together.

Conrad had grown up to be a sturdy, fearless boy who deeply admired his father. Othon had taught him to fight with a wooden sword, and the child could often be seen out on the grounds, fighting the invisible enemies that populated his imagination. Lidwine regularly invited her castellan friends, who lived in the village, to the castle, and these women were accompanied by their children. She also invited minstrels to the castle; they provided entertainment in the form of music or poetry. The cook also baked tasty cakes for them.

Conrad had very quickly expressed his desire to become the

leader of his playmates, which pleased the Duke of Sacht. At six years old, he hadn't yet left his parents' castle, but in time he would go live in another castle to become a page in the service of a knight. The knight would teach him to fight, to ride, to look after the horses, and even to serve food. All the boys of noble families were educated in this way.

Aysu had discovered these foreign customs in her native country, and she was delighted. She was startled, however, when Lidwine told her, "Did you know that Conrad is already engaged?"

"No. Is that possible, given that he's so young?"

"Yes, because some of our neighbors are trying to take our land. So, rather than go to war with them, we chose instead promise our son to their five-year-old daughter."

"And have they accepted?"

"Yes, and since then we've become friends."

"But if the marriage doesn't succeed, will the friendship end?"

"Rest easy: that rarely happens."

"And what if Conrad refuses this marriage? He already has a strong personality."

Lidwine seemed surprised by the question. "Unless the girl has some kind of hidden defect, he won't have the right to object. Besides, you know his mother, the marquise de Virlojeux; she visits me every Thursday afternoon. She wouldn't stand for that."

Aysu remained nonplussed, but made no comment.

At the end of 1203, before the Christmas festivities began, the young baroness felt tired. Rather than attend the many festivals organized between neighbors and friends to celebrate the Advent, she preferred to retire to her room

Surprised, Lidwine came looking for her. "Why don't you come see us anymore? I hope you're not angry with us?"

"Oh, no! Don't worry. You've all been so kind to me! But all the noise is making me a bit dizzy. I need to rest."

"Pardon me if I seem intrusive, but you're not pregnant, are you? That would be perfectly fine."

Aysu raised her eyes, which were bright with joy, to meet those of her sister-in-law. "I would be so happy if I was!"

Lidwine brought the matron who had delivered her own children, and the older woman confirmed that Aysu was indeed pregnant. The birth was expected to take place in May 1204. When Quentin heard the news, he felt both happy and worried: he was still haunted by the memory of Herminie's death....

After the Christmas festivities ended in January 1204, Quentin sent a letter to his friend Thibaut Menard, who lived at the castle, in Burgundy. These are the words Quentin used:

My dear friend,

I must inform you that, following a quarrel between my father and myself, it is no longer possible for me to reside in his fortress.

After participating in the Fourth Crusade in the Middle East, I took a new wife there. Opposing the marriage, my father chased us out of the fortress.

We're staying with my sister at the moment.

Also, with this letter, I'm asking you to put us up while we wait to find a solution. I'll explain everything to you in person.

Counting on your understanding and friendship as I await your decision.

Sincerely yours,

Quentin Lanicey

The young baron received a favorable response from Thibaut de Menard, and—after thanking his sister and the Duke for their kind hospitality—he asked the servants to pack up their luggage.

Aysu, who had befriended Lidwine, was secretly apprehensive

of this new beginning. But the important thing was that she went along with her husband, for he alone could reassure and protect her.

It was the Duke's coachman who drove the carriage. As they were travelling over a long distance, they had to spend several nights in a hostel. Once they arrived at Pouilly, in the duchy of Burgundy, they soon saw the castle where the Count of Menard lived. It had been built on a rocky outcrop at the end of the eleventh century, but its proportions remained modest. Initially, it had included a simple square tower; this was later joined by a solid enclosure, flanked by two round towers. The castle was reached by a drawbridge. Once inside, they saw a wide staircase spiral upward within a quadrangular tower.

Happy to see each other again, the two friends embraced each other tightly, laughing all the while. Quentin was astonished to find out that Thibaut—he who had charmed so many noble ladies in the past—was finally getting married!

"This is my wife, Brunilde. Last year, she gave me an adorable son, so now I have everything I wanted."

Brunilde was a beautiful young lady, very elegantly dressed, who probably originated from a wealthy family.

"Congratulations, dear Thibaut!" Quentin exclaimed. "I haven't been as lucky as you—my lovely Herminie, who you met, passed away during childbirth, and then I signed up for the Fourth Crusade. I found my new wife during the Crusade, in the lands of the former Byzantine Empire."

The count rushed over to Aysu and bowed deeply to her. "Noble lady, your beauty illuminates this castle. I'm delighted to meet you."

Aysu blushed slightly as she thanked him; she had the immediate impression that this man was seductive and fickle.

Thibaut had reserved a very nice room for them, tastefully furnished, whose windows overlooked an orchard. A maid helped the young baroness get settled. Aysu then she decided to rest, as the carriage ride had tired her out.

Meanwhile, the two friends—now settled comfortably in the reception hall—spoke freely, sipping good wine. Quentin explained why he had left his father. Godefroy latter was angry that he had dared to marry without his consent—or, rather, because he had not decided upon the marriage.

Thibaut was revolted by the sire's misconduct. How could he refuse a young woman as pretty as Aysu?

"That old bastard—pardon me for my language—is still obsessed with himself," the count declared.

"And he chased me out of my home, after threatening to disinherit me! What a terrible father! But for me, he's not my father anymore."

"If he disinherits you, where will you go?"

"I've given it some thought. My brother, the Duke of Sacht, has another fortress in Bavaria, which is currently unoccupied. If he agreed to give the fortress to me, I could manage it, but first he would have to do work to restore it. That's why I asked to stay with you for now."

"Yes, that could be a fitting solution."

"Are you planning on taking revenge for your father's unforgivable arrogance?" Thibaut asked.

"No, not yet, but if I did, that would comfort me."

For a short time, they were both immersed in their own thoughts. Then, Thibaut asked, "Actually, my friend, you haven't told me how you have avenged your stepmother. Remember how she deigned to refuse my advances at your wedding with your first wife?"

"That's true. Well, I must tell you: she died from an accident—an unlucky fall from her horse. A huge stone broke away from the cliff, right in front of the horse, and the horse reared up. She fell on her head and did not survive. When the snow melts, it's not uncommon for rocks to fall off the cliff and cause accidents like this."

"My God! Can it be?" the count cried. "So, has fate avenged you after all?"

"Yes, and I must admit that I wasn't upset."

"Then we've both had our revenge. Excellent!"

They continued to drink, and—under the influence of so much alcohol—they both started laughing.

Like Quentin, Thibaut of Menard was a strong supporter of King Otto IV of Brunswick. He had friends who were close to the king. One such friend was Odo III, Duke of Burgundy, who had married a relative of Otto IV. He often the Duke's palace in Dijon to attend the many festivals that he organized to entertain his friends in high places.

The duke dragged Quentin and his wife, who were welcomed into this social circle, to the castle. The young baron was pleased to find his old friend, Roland Chessac, and they entertained themselves by dueling with their swords, as they had when they were twenty. However, the Countess of Chessac—who had once been in love with Quentin—felt a pang of jealousy upon seeing his wife's radiant beauty.

The Duke organized hunting parties with hounds, as well as tournaments. The tournaments brought over a great many knights, not only from Burgundy, but also from faraway places like Flanders and Germany, and even England.

As they sat, talking, in their living rooms, these aristocrats were quite concerned with politics, both from France and Germany.

It was at one such party where Thibaut and Quentin came into contact with a German prince who had married a Burgundian countess. The prince, who was a strong supporter of Otto IV of Brunswick, excited him so much that they decided to fight by his side. The first step was to warn Otto's opponents, a group to which the baron of Lanicey and his friends belonged. Then, the second step consisted in attacking them—and thus weakening—them.

Thibaut told Quentin, "My friend, you'll have an excellent alibi if you take revenge on your father."

"What do you mean?"

"Well, if you tell the truth to the supporters of this German prince, they won't hesitate to besiege his fortress. And since there are a lot of them, it's very likely that the baron of Lanicey will be defeated."

"I need some time to think," Quentin replied right away.

The young baron hated his father, naturally, as the latter had banned him from the castle. But to attack his fortress, and perhaps destroy it.... That solution seemed terrible. Quentin had grown up in that castle, and lived there until quite recently.

Back in Pouilly, Thibaut asked him again: "Have you been thinking about attacking your father's castle? Remember that opposing Othon is an act of treason, and he must be punished for that."

Quentin hesitated once more before saying, "You're right. But I don't want him to die."

"Bah! He'll know how to defend himself. He's an old fox, believe me. And remember that he chased me off the premises during your first marriage."

The young man finally agreed, but he refused to join the fighters.

Spring was beginning to hang tender buds on the trees; nature itself seemed to be waking up. The first crocus pierced the snows that blanked the ground, yellow daffodils invaded the woods, and wild herbs were beginning to escape the stony paths. The peasants were getting ready to plow the ground.

Godefroy sometimes walked on his land, but he still spent much of his time in the castle, managing his accounts or writing letters. One day, while in his study, he heard galloping noises, mixed with the neighing of horses. Looking outside, he noticed that riders on horseback were getting uncommonly close to his fortress, even though he wasn't expecting anyone.

Intrigued, he climbed on top of the tower and addressed the guards. "In the distance, I see many unknown riders; this doesn't bode well. What do you think?"

"You are correct, my lord. The riders are certainly armed men who want to attack you."

"Make sure everyone us ready to fight back!" he ordered. "Remove the drawbridge, and fast!

A rumor that the enemies were drawing near spread quickly among the castle's inhabitants, and the panicked maids began to cry. The servants, meanwhile, were running in all directions. Only Ulric kept his composure. Joining the sire, he saw that many warriors had surrounded the fortress, and they were shouting.

"Down with the Lord Lanicey, the traitor who refuses to obey our king!" declared their flag bearer. "We know that he conspired to help the usurper Philip of Swabia, and it's for that reason that we will tear him down!"

"You have nothing to fear, Master," Ulric said firmly. "They will tire before we do. Even if they besiege us, we can live here for a long time before we'll need to go out and get supplies. We have enough food and water."

"No, I don't care," said the sire. "Have you made sure that all the exits are closed?"

"Yes, they all are."

"So we have to wait until they get tired. Still, go check if we have enough food to resist them."

Thus, for almost a fortnight, the fortress's inhabitants did not leave the castle. A guard told Godefroy that an enemy had tried to bribe him; he had offered him a large sum of money against opening the door. But, maintaining his integrity, the guard refused the offer.

If they managed to defeat these felons, the sire promised the guard, then he would raise his rank. He had recognized these warriors as belonging to the clan of Otto IV of Brunswick.

Given that the sire did not surrender after fifteen days of siege, the attackers decided to change tactics. They tried to dig a tunnel under the perimeter wall, supporting it with stones and wooden beams, with the goal of making the wall collapse. They dug for many hours, but Godefroy remained calm; he knew that this wall had been built on a rock that was three meters thick. Thus, it was impossible to access the castle this way.

Next, they used ballistae—large crossbows, mounted on legs with wheels, which were strong enough to launch giant arrows for several meters. But the sire's guards had ballistae as well. Dozens of arrows, coming from both sides of the perimeter wall, flew on top of the wall. Unfortunately, during the battle, many of the fortress's warriors were hit and killed, which greatly agitated the people on both sides. Then, using a tower known as a belfry, the traitors decided to climb the along the wall. The belfry was a wooden tower on wheels, covered with wet pelts so that it would be flammable. The tower allowed the traitors to climb while remaining protected. Its height had been calculated so that it would dominate over top of a wall, and so that its floors could harbor a great many attackers.

The lord ordered his men to drive back the tower. It collapsed, but, by that time, several of the attackers had managed to reach the top of the wall. They jumped inside the courtyard and eviscerated the front door with an axe. They used their swords to massacre the other soldiers in the castle, and then managed to get inside. Finally, grabbing a torch hanging from the wall, one of the attackers used it to set fire to the curtains. The fabric burned quickly, but Ulric managed to put it out by throwing a bucket of water onto it. Ambushing the invaders from behind a staircase, a few brave soldiers launched their arrows at them, but several were killed in the ensuing attack. The other warriors then fled, along with the servants, thanks to an exit that was hidden behind a wardrobe.

Thus, the attackers remained locked inside the fortress, but—considering themselves victorious—they cried out with joy. Their leader, a lord belonging to the clan of Otto IV, said, "Our mission will not be complete until we have found the sire of the castle, dead or alive. If he's still alive, we'll capture him and drag him before king's court. The king will decide what sentence should be given to him."

"Hurrah!" the winning warriors shouted. "Let's look for him! We'll search this fortress from top to bottom until we get our hands on him. That way, the traitor will no doubt remember us!"

They penetrated all the rooms in the castle, breaking chairs and dishes as they went. Some also took the opportunity to steal the valuables in the fortress. At last, they all found themselves in the main room, dragging with them a few poor women who had not managed to escape in time. Among these women was old Hilda, who did not fear death. The leader rushed at her, and, pointing his sword under his throat, commanded her, "You, old woman, tell us where your master is hiding, or I'll cut your throat."

Without trembling, Hilda simply replied, "My lord, we do not know...because our master never tells us where he goes when he's not in the fortress."

All of a sudden, fifty armed soldiers ran, screaming, into the room. They had come in via an exit that was known only to the Baron of Lanicey.

"You're trapped like rats! This is it!" he roared.

With the help of his friends—the Viscount of Palindrey, the Marquis of Attrans, and the Count of Fouchardière—he could easily massacre all these felons.